IAN WOODHEAD

# GALACTIC TROOPERS

SEVERED PRESS
HOBART TASMANIA

# GALACTIC TROOPERS

# CHAPTER ONE

In another two more minutes, that punishment drone would be floating past his cell door. Ex-Trooper, Danny Cole, previously of the strike-down unit and posted to the Imperial heavy cruiser, *The Donnington Scimitar*, now labelled as a minor heretic, rolled his collected prize in the palm of his filthy hand.

He didn't have enough moss. Trooper Cole was going to need at least double the amount to even have a chance of his desperate plan to succeed. Apart from the ceiling, which he could not reach, he had scraped the four walls down to the bare stone. He bet this cell hadn't been this clean for over two hundred years.

One more minute to go.

There was no other choice in this. Mr. Smith would have to lose some weight.

"You can't do that to me, buddy boy! If I vanish, you'll have nobody left to look after you. Who's going to be here when you wake up screaming from your nightmares? You seriously need to think about this."

Trooper Cole was taken aback by this rather unusual outburst. He'd never heard the voice of reason be so vocal before. "Calm your jets, I'll only be taking some of you." He moved past his stone-slab bed and stopped in front of the two-metre-high, crude, human-shaped outline. "What needs to be done, needs to be done." Trooper Cole dug his finger into the narrow gap between two stone blocks and managed to pick out a sizeable lump of moss which he added to his collection. It worried him not to hear Mr. Smith bitterly complaining about Trooper Cole poking holes in his outline. He guessed the voice of reason was probably sulking.

1

He had thirty seconds left. Trooper Cole crouched and furiously scraped off as much moss as he dare within his now rapidly shrinking time period. Did he have enough? Well, Trooper Cole would soon find out. He raced over to the cell door and pressed his nose between the bars in the large window.

The distant sound of the vile creature's incessant beeping made his heart skip a beat. He couldn't remember the last time he had been this excited. Oh wait, yes he did. Last month, the guards served all the prisoners with real food. The rumour he heard was their glorious Empire had wiped the hateful insectoid Blanik fighters off the face of their home planet. Trooper Cole didn't believe that propaganda nonsense at all. He kept his opinions to himself and sat on his slab and ate something which resembled a carrot, if he squinted.

The punishment drone had risen up to his level now. He listened to the other prisoners shouting at it, calling the thing dirty names. One prisoner even spat at the drone when it floated past his cell door. The poor bugger received a stream of neural inhibitors for his trouble. Trooper Cole could swear that the globule of wet snot made a fizzing noise when it landed on its battered outer casing. This plan was going to work, he knew it.

"You're going to die, you rash fool. Come back to the slab, buddy boy, and bring me back my legs. They'll be signing the release forms any day now."

"Piss off, Mr. Smith," he muttered. There would be no pardon for this minor heretic, no matter how badly their side was doing in this civil war. They were going to make an example of him. In three days' time, the guards would drag him from this dank cell, up to the surface, and epoxy his naked body to a twelve-metre pole in Traitor's Corner before the captain of the *Donnington Scimitar* boiled his brain with a single shot from his ship-issued sidearm.

Trooper Cole's plan was as simple as it was devious. Everyone knew that these ancient drones should have been scrapped hundreds of years ago. The damn things were even built way before the Third Reformation. Suffice to say, they were running on spit and luck, but not prisoner's spit, obviously. If he could get this ball of wet stinking material down the drone's intake vent, it might malfunction. His hope, if he was in the mood for a proper fairy tale, is that the drone would fall to the floor outside his cell door and explode, with the resulting after effect of his door unlocking and swinging open.

"That is not going to happen," said the voice of reason. "You can't escape from here; nobody can."

Trooper Cole hated it when Mr. Smith crawled through his private thoughts like a Tazkhanion slug.

"The best you can hope for is a blast from its phaser coil, knocking you out until they come to melt your ragged body. If you do this, you can kiss goodbye to any thought of a pardon."

The drone was now three doors away. "If that is my fate, then bring it on." Trooper Cole turned and glared at what remained of the moss outline on the far wall. "It means that I won't have to listen to your whining voice ever again. It also means that the dreams will finally be over, Mr. Smith."

"Do you not find it annoying that you can never remember your dreams?"

Trooper Cole heard the sly undertones of that last statement, but he chose to ignore it. Mr. Smith's scare tactics weren't going to work on him, no way. He'd stopped worrying about the contents of his dreams months ago.

He carefully picked up the tightly rolled ball of moss and got ready to throw it. The drone was now two doors from his cell. Just to be able to get a good night's sleep without those insidious dreams tearing into his soul was enough reason to let them kill him. He looked down at his moss and suppressed a hysterical giggle. There was no way this dumb plan would work, not that this was going to stop him from trying.

"Goodbye, my voice of reason. I would say that it's been a pleasure knowing you, but it hasn't. With luck, the afterlife will be a little kinder to me than this one has." The drone had now stopped outside the cell door next to his.

He then realised just how much he'd also miss his cellmate. The Gizanti in the next room had been his only friend in here, about from Mr. Smith, that is. In fact, without the Gizanti's frequent interventions during rest period and exercise hour, Trooper knew he wouldn't be alive now to attempt this stupid escape.

His voice of reason was now chuckling. "Are you sure you don't want to abort this ridiculous escape plan? See, I suspect that your slow mind has just reached the part of what to do if, by some miracle, your plan to get out of here does work."

The Gizanti, Trooper Cole, and whole other bunch of freaks on this level were classed as political prisoners. The guard kept them locked up for most of the time while the rest of the population were allowed free reign on the hell level. He'd have to pass through that first before somehow thinking of a way to break into the guard admin section.

The Gizanti hurled a stream of abuse in the common tongue at the drone, and the machine responded by blasting the huge armour-plated creature with a neural inhibitor. As the inhibitor was calibrated for human brains, it had no effect on the alien, and nobody had bothered to reprogram the drone to account for the fact that humans were the only intelligent life-form in this galaxy after all.

His cellmate smashed his heavy frame against the cell door, which resulted in yet another blast from the drone. Trooper Cole realised he could be waiting for some time. It was rare for the Gizanti to be so vocal.

He had wondered how long it would take before the big guy's temper finally broke. From the crashing and banging coming from the other cell, he guessed that the human jailers' thoughts of a quiet night had well and truly gone into the trash compactor. Give it a few more minutes, and those muscle-enhanced idiots would be up here with their electro-batons and sleep sprayers. Trooper Cole was watching his escape plan peel away at the seams and he was helpless to stop it. What could have so upset the Gizanti? Granted, it wasn't exactly the most pleasant of individuals, but on most occasions, he just found most of the human dramas going on inside here funny.

"Perhaps if you had kept your ears open instead of obsessing over your ridiculous escape plan, you might understand the reason," said his voice of reason. "The drone spoke to the Gizanti in its native tongue, Trooper Cole."

"What did it say?"

"How am I going to know that, you idiot? Surely your psychosis hasn't reached the level where you and I have totally split apart?"

The Gizanti was still shouting at the drone, but it was no longer banging about. It had switched to it native language now too. Trooper Cole had the feeling that the drone had pushed the alien a little too far today. Not that it would have taken that much. All Gizanti had an inbuilt hatred for machine intelligence. On their world, everything from drones to weapons to starships had to be vat grown.

"If we do go our separate ways, does that mean I get to choose my own name? Oh, I won't have you stealing my moss anymore either."

"Shut up."

A week before the misunderstanding at Praxis Three Spaceport, which resulted in the local priest accusing him of heresy, Trooper Cole and his squad attended a weapons training programme. The sergeant in charge had allowed him to bond with a Gizanti pulse blaster. He'd found it most disconcerting to listen to the weapon politely asking Trooper Cole to move his fingers as the pulse blaster was uncomfortable with his alien paws being so close to its anal vent.

When Trooper Cole heard two more drones rising to this level, he should have guessed the jailers wouldn't have bothered checking this out in person. They cared too much about their card game than the apparent safety of their prisoners. He guessed it matter whether human or electronic eyes arrived next door, his slim chance of escaping had now dropped to zero. Once the Gizanti saw the additional metal blasphemies, he was going to go absolutely crazy with rage.

Silently admitting defeat was difficult, but even he knew when to quit. Trooper Cole retreated to the wall, he crouched and began to rebuild Mr. Smith. There would even be some left to give his voice of reason a pair of kneecaps. "It's nice to know it wasn't a complete waste of time." He looked up. "Are you not going to say that I told you so, Mr. Smith? It's so unlike you to miss an opportunity to insult me."

Trooper Cole applied the moss while listening as the screams in the next cell restarted once the two drones joined their companion. It sounded cruel, but he wished their neural inhibitor did work on his species. At this rate, the Gizanti would be spending the rest of the night in the torture tank.

"I implore that you lie down now before it is too late. It will soon be starting, Trooper Cole!"

There was no sign of that humorous tone now. Mr. Smith was deadly serious about his request. Well, stuff Mr. Smith, he wasn't going to take notice of anything he was going to say to him tonight, not after the zero encouragement his voice of reason he gave to him. It's almost as if he didn't want Trooper Cole to try to escape. Mr. Smith hadn't even thanked him for redoing his body.

He stood up, wiped the remaining bits of moss down the side of his trousers, then stood back to admire the improvements he'd made. He'd obviously been wasted as a squad leader in one of the most ruthless assassination units in the Mighty Terran Empire. Trooper Cole should have been one of those eccentric artists travelling from planet to planet. Judging by what he'd done with Mr. Smith, he would have made a fortune!

The screaming in the next cell increased in volume, so did the sounds of the three drones hurting the big guy. They were using their own version of the human electro-baton on the big guy. At this rate, those metal bastards would end up cracking open the Gizanti's thick orange hide.

Though the screams, he heard a few words in the common tongue. It was difficult to make out what the Gizanti was saying at first, but as he repeated the phrase over and over, Trooper Cole began to understand what the first drone had said and the reason for his cellmate's violent reaction. He was saying that everyone on home-world had been stolen.

He heard the three electro-batons strike the creature's plating, yet it felt like him who had just been attacked. Every muscle in his body seized up, the motion toppled him, and he crashed onto the floor. He never even felt the impact as his mind had taken him somewhere else.

Trooper Cole found himself standing on the edge of a high cliff. A man of the same height as him stood a couple of paces to his left. The other man turned his head, and Trooper Cole found himself staring at his own face just about a decade older.

"You're me?"

"I'm Mr. Smith," he replied, "and welcome to your dream. You're going to wish that you did as he asked, Trooper Cole, as this is so going to hurt you."

# CHAPTER TWO

He heard the glikgliks before his flock even uttered their panicked bleating. Walish Din snapped open his eyes, launched his wiry frame out of his hammock, grabbed the staff, and raced out of the small tent. The two moons gave the young Diannin enough light to see just how close his twelve animals had wandered to the edge of the canyon.

"You tiny-brained, seven-legged morons!" he yelled, racing towards his flock. "Get back down here or you'll feel the end of my staff on your heads!" His threats would make no difference. They all heard the shepherd and uttered the panicked bleating that Walish Din heard moments before, but none retreated from the edge. Why go back to barren land when the grass pods here were so plentiful and delicious?

If just one of those animals fell into the basin, both his spawn donors would elect to have Walish Din pushed back into the group shell. He shuddered at that dire thought. Yet the mental threat, even if it was partially of his own making, helped to push his legs a little harder.

He reached the first animal, grabbed her hind tusks, and propelled the stupid animal behind him, hoping the rest of them would follow her. Walish Din ground his teeth in frustration when not one of the animals took any notice of one of their own rolling down the steep incline like a large seed wheel. It just meant more tasty grass pods for them to munch!

Walish Din had to use his full repertoire of command words and thought strings to get the annoying animals to move away from the grass pods. He threaded his way through his flock, tapping the more stubborn animal with the staff to ensure they kept moving. There was one glikglik who hadn't stopped stuffing the grass pods into her guts. "Come down here, you pain in the glipharg!"

She looked down from her perch, gave the shepherd a defiant bleat, before continuing to graze on the grass pods clinging to the side of the rock.

"I hate my life," he said, dropping the staff so he could climb using both hands. "I hate my spawn donors." It wasn't fair that he should look after these idiotic animals when his spawn kin were allowed to leave the nest and grow their own farms. Walish Din was now just a few inches away from the remaining animal. "I'm warning you! Get down here right now, or I'll push you over myself!" Just because he possessed the touch, just because he could connect with their minds without the use of flock tendrils. "Most of all," he gasped, reaching for the stray glikglik, "I hate you!"

Walish Din grabbed the animal's hind tusk and held on, despite her reaching around and trying to bite his fingers. "No you don't!" He gave the beast a vicious tug, felling victorious when the glikglik lost her grip and tumbled down the rock. His victory quickly turned to guilt when he saw that two of her legs were now badly twisted. It would take a good three nights for them to heal. He watched her limp over to the rest of the flock, wondering how he was going to explain this to his spawn donors when the sun kissed the two moons.

To make his situation even more ridiculous and annoying, Walish Din wasn't too sure how to get back down. The only way he could go appeared to be up. He held onto the rocks then looked down, trying to work out how he climbed up here. Getting the glikglik down had been had been his only concern; consequently, Walish Din hadn't been watching where he placed his feet. "You're more stupid than the glikgliks."

His only option was to climb higher and hoped that once he reached the top, he might be able to see another way down. He sighed heavily, wishing he had stayed in his tent now. Walish Din carefully climbed up the rock while wondering if his spawn donors really would elect to have him stuffed back into the group shell if he had allowed some of the flock to fall down into the canyon basin. At this rate, the only creature likely to fall to their death was going to be him.

The shepherd felt this was his life-changing moment. When he finally got back down to solid ground, Walish Din was going to tell his spawn donors and the tribe elders that he no longer had the touch. It's not like they could prove otherwise. The tips of his fingers found another lip on the rock face. It felt sturdy enough. There was another lip a little higher too. He prayed to the Gods, then let go of the crumbly stuff under his other hand and swung his body to the left, knowing that if that lip wasn't as solid as he hoped, he would be following that stubborn glikglik. Unlike the animal, Walish Din would not be limping away.

His fingers managed to grab the other lip, and he had to use all of his remaining strength to pull himself up. He had done it though; Walish Din had reached the summit. His hope was now that he was reasonably secure, he would be able to map a way back to his flock and his tent. He was so missing his hammock.

There was a way down that didn't involve leaping off the top, although that thought had crossed his mind. After all, it wasn't that far down to the ground, perhaps the height of one of the alien buildings in the centre of the settlement. Unlike the other side, where if he fell that way, his body would be shredded on the sharp rocks before what was left of him even splatted into the basin, hundreds of feet below.

Walish Din's morbid curiosity got the better of him, and instead of looking for the handholds and footholds, which must have used to get up here, he looked over on the other side. Every single one of the shepherd's synapses misfired at the sight of the standing bodies covering the basin floor.

"What is this?" He held onto the rock as tight as he dare without it slicing into his flesh while trying to come to terms with what this could be. He shut his eyes, counted to ten, then opened them again, groaning when he discovered he wasn't imagining seeing thousands and thousands of alien people down there.

He lowered himself into a lying position, attempted to calm his secondary heart, and tried to work out how best he could describe what he saw once Walish Din returned to his tribe. His spawn donors and the elders would need to know every detail. Was this an invasion?

His eyes were keen, another reason why they gave him this the boring job of tending glikgliks. Still, perhaps he shouldn't complain too bitterly. After all, thanks to him, his tribe would now know about this invasion before any of the other Diannin tribes scattered across the surface of this planet. He focused on the statue-like figures closest to the edge of the basin. He frowned. They were human. He was sure of it. There were a few of that species who had built shops in the centre of the settlement.

Walish Din didn't know much about the species, but he was sure that they didn't go around invading planets, certainly not one as backward as the dirt-ball he had the misfortune of being spawned upon. These were different to the traders in town. For a start, the traders moved about, and none of the humans in town had bits of metal and what looked like dozens of wires attached to their flesh.

The humans were all grouped into huge circles, each one containing hundreds of individuals. He counted thirty of these circles across the canyon basin. Another species surrounded the humans, one that Walish Din had never seen in the settlement. They were truly frightening. The creatures towered over the humans by at least a foot. Thick orange-plated armour covered the creature from head to tail. Just like the humans, they too were immobile and had strips of metal and wires attached to them.

Walish Din decided that he had seen enough of this unearthly wonder. Smarter Diannin minds were needed to unlock this puzzle, and his instinct as well as his touch told him that this vast collection of statue-like aliens were not going to vanish anytime soon. How much longer would they stay inactive?

He did not know exactly what the elders would ask of him once Walish Din was allowed to speak in their presence. Perhaps it would be best to ensure he saw everything that needed seeing before running to them.

"Listen to yourself, like those old fools knew anything about alien activities." He did have a point there. They might be experts on milking the farmain orchards and glikglik breeding methods, but when it came to off-world activities, those idiots were about as knowledgeable as the glikgliks down there, now grazing close to his tent.

Still, it would not be proper to return without every scrap of information he could glean from this bizarre sight. He took his eyes off his flock and reluctantly looked back at the canyon basin. Not all the humans were surrounded by the orange dragons. He wasn't sure if that was important, but he remembered it anyway.

His glikgliks had started bleating again; they had probably run out of grass pods. Walish Din turned around, intending to shout at the stupid things, when he saw they were all looking up at the sky.

He followed their gaze and cried out when several bright lights shot through the thick cloud cover, heading straight for the canyon basin. The lights smashed into the earth, and once the dust had returned to the ground, another orange dragon, complete with the metal additions, appeared at the edge of the humans. The lights continued to streak through the sky, each one adding another dragon to the collection of aliens down there.

Walish Din had seen enough. He had to get out of this place. Right now, the shepherd just wanted to run home and take shelter under the earth.

The number of lights were increasing, their illumination changing night into day. Surely, he could not be the only one who was witnessing this? Yet, Walish Din saw no movement from either his settlement or from the town.

He tried to swallow down the lump of fear that was lodged in his throat and started to look for a safe way down, to see if he could map a route. Walish Din turned and lowered his legs over the edge, holding onto a lump of jutting-out rocks while his left foot managed to find a gap large enough for him to lower his body down a few inches.

Walish Din whimpered and sobbed as he continued to move down the rock face, while his flock of glikgliks sounded like they were bleating out encouragement. It didn't shock him in the slightest to see they were now directly beneath him. "I don't like this at all!"

The lights still rained down, each one vanishing behind the rock to strike the canyon basin. He now believed that whatever life he once had would soon be well and truly over. He was witnessing what could be the end of his world as well as the end his spawn donors' comfortable lives as well. The glikgliks were now beginning to panic, only the ones underneath him weren't. Walish Din stopped climbing down, flattened his body against the rock face, and held on with all his might as the touch slammed into him.

He saw dozens of those lights veering away from the basin. They struck the ground close to his settlement and the town. Walish Din's eyeballs rolled up into the sockets. For the first time since connection, the touch severed the cord between him and his flock before taking his spirit far across the planet, and into the only city on the Diannin planet which possessed a working spaceport. From there, he heard himself screaming in terror as his spirit took him from his own planet, across the blackness of space, before depositing him onto the surface of a strange world. Walish Din had no time to marvel at this impossibility as, just like on his world, similar events were happening here. He saw dozens of aliens and humans all running for their lives as the lights smashed into buildings, roads, and vehicles. The orange dragons emerged from the rubble and the twisted metal. Walish Din's spirit stood in the midst of a food establishment and listened to humans and tall, blue, hairless aliens gasp as these monsters all pulled long, thick silver poles from off their backs. Just like the monsters, grey wire wrapped around the surface of the devices.

His spirit pushed Walish Din closer to the store window. He found himself next to a human female. She had long blonde hair and bright blue eyes. Just like everybody else in the food establishment, her gaze was fixed upon the closest orange dragon. He heard a couple of humans calling them Gizanti. An old human male standing beside the female was shaking his head in disbelief. He was telling everybody that they could not be Gizanti, as those big orange bastards grew all their own gear.

His remaining words were drowned out as everybody screamed in horror when the orange dragon aimed the long device at a group of young blue aliens who were racing across the road. A stream of blue fire erupted from the end and incinerated the fleeing creatures.

Walish Din wept. His spirit showed him their last journey towards the Plains of Gopin as the orange dragon lumbered away from the front of the shop. He didn't want to be here anymore. The shepherd wished he hadn't opened his big stupid mouth to ask for something more exciting than tending his flock of stupid glikgliks.

"You need to make your way to the city, Walish Din."

Was she speaking to him? Of course she was; the female had said his name. She looked directly at him and repeated her words.

"You can see me?"

"I'm not here and neither are you. Get to the city, young Diannin, and get off this world. There is no need to tend to your flock anymore, shepherd. I'm also afraid to tell you that there won't even be time to tend to your grief either."

The girl then did something utterly bizarre. She leaned towards him and pressed her lips against his mouth.

"You have to come here and find me, Walish Din. You need to find me before the other one arrives."

"What other one?"

"I only know he's called Danny. Come here. Find me before it's too late!"

Walish Din's eyes opened and he found himself looking up into the sky. The lights were still hitting the ground. Sounds of distant screaming reached him. He turned his head and saw flames rising from his settlement. He knew the orange dragons with their Godlike weapons were now stomping through the narrow streets, killing anyone that moved.

"No!" he yelled.

His flock bleated below him. The girl's words echoed through his head, and Walish Din pulled one hand away from the rock-face. He said a silent prayer for his spawn donors who were now surely wandering through the Plains of Gopin before he took his remaining hand off the rock.

# CHAPTER THREE

Philip Diocolis, Prime Chaplain of the Third Imperial Order, watched impassively while hordes of strange alien grey orbs streaked across the surface of the Gizanti home planet. The terrified local population scattered in every direction, some seeking shelter under their living vehicles, some falling to the floor and curling up inside their armour plating. It didn't make any difference. When the orbs flew over the creatures, a sick yellow light emerged from under the orb and the Gizantis disappeared.

This had been the fourth time that he had watched the newest recording. Just like the past three occasions, he wanted to dismiss this as a piece of ridiculous fiction. Something vomited from the mind of some raving lunatic whose only future contribution to the empire would be when his composted body enriches the roses in the royal garden.

The Prime Chaplain gave the silent command and took a small sip of his meat broth while he waited for the forward monitor's extra viewing screens to fold out. To even contemplate that The God-Emperor was no longer the only human in the galaxy with the revered gift would be suicide, even for a subject as highly placed as himself. If word got out that he took these dreams seriously, he would likely be sharing the same cell as the ex-Trooper Cole.

"Run comparisons again. Time index fourteen point six on both versions. Remove emotive interference and restore primal designation on just the Imperial copy this time."

He watched the two recordings again. The scenario on the left, taken from the feverish mind of their young God-Emperor, while the scene playing beside it was recorded at the exact moment, yet this one came from the sleeping mind of the minor heretic.

"And there is total surety regarding the origins of both recordings."

"There is no disambiguation. The sources correspond," replied the soft voice of the priest's personal index.

Did he just detect an undertone of indignation hidden within that electronic voice? No, that was ridiculous. His mind was obviously playing tricks on him, making him believe that he had upset her feelings by suggesting she had mixed up the recordings.

The Chaplain's mind certainly wasn't playing tricks on him when it came to the implications of what this meant for the future of the greatest empire in the galaxy. The Chaplain sighed to himself. Even that 'fact' no longer rang true.

To think that only eight days before he, like most Imperial citizens, believed that the will of the God-Emperor would never be broken by the Empire's many enemies, whether alien or from the increasing armies of human heretics. Unlike the ordinary citizen, he knew exactly the terrors and threats the Empire faced, and yet his conviction in his faith and the Emperor was absolute. At least, that was the case until exactly one week before.

Being summoned to attend a gathering with the Revered Holy Order, headed by the High Priestess herself, had not been how he expected to begin his day. The Prime Chaplain anticipated that they were to give him another post within the Holy Office. It was something he had been expecting for over two years. It was about time that the Revered Holy Order recognising his due diligence with a promotion.

His dreams of a larger congregation as well as hopes of a chance to join the Holy Order was promptly shattered when the woman, second only to the God Emperor, told Philip that an unknown alien force had penetrated the outer defences of two minor Imperial agrarian planets and depopulated the surface.

She suggested that this unprecedented threat could become humanity's downfall. Just to hear the High Priestess utter such blasphemy had shaken the Prime Chaplain's faith to the very core. Looking back to his tumultuous thoughts once he had received his executive orders, as well as the Priestess giving him special dispensation, perhaps it had been best to allow such impure ideas run their strange course. Whilst still within the chambers of the apostolic palace, there was still a chance of the very walls to cleanse him.

"Run the recordings again, Index. Overlay both using the Gizanti vehicle as the reference point." The Index acknowledged his command. He leaned forward, watching one more time as these unknown orbs streaked across the alien sky, disintegrating every life form on the surface. Just as the Prime Chaplain suspected, the two recordings were not taken from the same perspective.

This was all the verification he needed. The minor heretic would not be facing a firing squad after all, although ex-Trooper Cole might be very well wish he had kissed traitor's pole once Philip had done with him. It had been possible that the prisoner could have been picking up the Emperor's original vision, distorting the original source while enhancing the copy. The theory was, at best, a highly improbable hypothesis, but it still needed verification.

The Empire had found another prophet. The Prime Chaplain took a deep breath, then grabbed the arms of his ornate chair in the hope that a connection with an artefact from the Second Reformation might help to steady his nerves.

"Did she know?"

"More data is required before the question can be answered."

"Be quiet, Index."

The threat from a potentially superior technologically advanced aggressive alien species obviously wasn't enough for the Empire to deal with. The creator had to supply them with another prophet as well, one, from the single recording the Prime Chaplain had witnessed, made their God-Emperor look as revered as an Elasion slow worm.

The Prime Chaplain gripped the arms of the chair even harder after realising what he had just almost said aloud. No special dispensation would help him if the holy inquisitors had heard him commit high blasphemy. Yet, the facts, the pure unadulterated facts were there in front of him. Ex-Trooper Cole had indeed seen the future in his dreams. There could be no doubt.

"Index, separate the recordings. Focus on the sequence beginning with the first alien disintegration and ending with the orbs leaving the surface."

The Prime Chaplain frowned at the lack of monitor activity. His heartbeat quickened and his blood pressure rose in response. They must have heard, the order of the Inquisition had heard his blasphemy even now; they were coming for him.

He swallowed hard, telling himself that he was mistaken. "Index," he said, running his tongue across his dry lips. "Index, explain the reason for non-function."

"New data from the superior recording suggests the Gizanti were not disintegrated."

"I don't understand. What else could have happened to them?"

"Displacement is the only logical answer."

Philip almost burst out laughing. "No, that is totally impossible. There is nothing that can transport a population of two billion individuals from one place and another." He stood up and strode over to the monitor, peering at the frozen image of the Gizanti under that vehicle, seconds before the beam hit the creature. "Index, recompile all data, state that your previous statement was an error."

"There is no error."

Was his mind and body capable of any more shocks? "Index, replay recordings from Imperial archives grouped within Zenus Incident." He watched the two other scenarios pulled from the God-Emperor's mind. Like the Gizanti world, the orbs stripped away the human populations of each world within a solar day. The poor resolution and grainy quality made it difficult to discover how the alien orbs could disable the planets' defences with ease. Even if the Prime Chaplain did have the similar recordings from the minor heretic, he doubted just visual data would solve that particular problem. "Index, extrapolate theory that human populations could still live, based on the data taken from the superior recording."

"No data available."

No surprises there. Even if there was a possibility of the Imperial citizens still being alive, then surely he should give priority to their return priority to their safe return before seeking out the source of these orbs.

"Index, based on available information, is it possible that theses orbs could have displaced the Imperial citizens to a location in the vicinity of the three affected star systems?"

"No data available."

"There must be a viable planet close to the three systems that is large enough to sustain such a large amount of people."

"No data available."

"Fuck!"

The Prime Chaplain removed the papal key from within the folds of his ceremonial uniform, given to him by the Priestess earlier. He ran his fingers along the smooth edges. Did he have enough new information to contact her? He looked at the still images of one of these orbs floating just above one of the planet's inhabitants. Even with the poor quality image, it was not difficult to seen to look of pure terror upon that citizen's face.

Philip pushed the papal key into the slot in the chair arm and composed himself. He was Prime Chaplain; his duty was to the Emperor and to the billions of Imperial citizens, spread across an empire of almost two hundred planets.

The air by his side shimmered as the image of the High Priestess appeared before him. Her promptness started Philip. He had not expected her to be actually waiting. He jumped out of the chair, almost tripping up over his robe as he fell to the floor and pressed his forehead to the sacred symbol of justice, embossed on the polished grey stone, next to the chair.

"Glory be to the Empire and our revered Emperor," he said. "May his reign last for another thousand years."

The Prime Chaplain sneaked a sly gaze when she didn't immediately return the required response. Was she choking? Had Philip said something wrong? He wasn't sure how much more of this his poor heart could take.

The Priestess blinked then gave the Chaplain a smile that almost burst his already battered heart.

"You said that without a hint of irony. Congratulations. Now, am I to understand that you have an update?"

The Prime Chaplain did not understand that, so he brushed it to the back of his mind. Instead, he composed himself while he did his best to study the most desirable woman in the Empire without being seen.

The holographic image of the second most powerful figure in the Terran Empire turned her head to converse with a minion not visible. It gave him the opportunity to study her closer. Nobody knew her true age. The High Priestess had stayed looking like a young woman in her early twenties for over a hundred years. The fact that she should now resemble a feeble old crone did not stop millions of teenage males lusting after her. Of course, they kept their thoughts to themselves. To openly boast about what they could do with her full figure, long legs, and platinum blonde curly hair would likely end in lashes in a punishment square. He did know that the High Priestess did take lovers on a regular basis, but none of them lived to recant their exploits once she became bored of them.

On this occasion, she wore a sparkling pale cream shawl, with what hinted to be a dark green skin hugging dress underneath. If he was of sound mind and was not terrified that his very existence hinged on his next few words, the Prime Chaplain would have rather enjoyed the sight.

"Do you wish me to remove the shawl so you can take a closer look, Philip?"

He reddened. The Prime Chaplain thought she had read his mind until he released he'd been staring. "My apologies, I was—"

"I know what you were doing," she interrupted. "Do you have anything new to report or are you purposely wasting my time?"

"With the additional recordings, I can announce that the human and Zaginti populations were not disintegrated," he said. "The available evidence does suggest that the aggressors could have displaced them." He paused and tried not to allow his nervousness to show. She wanted more; she was waiting for him to continue. At this rate, it was he who would end up being disintegrated. "The aliens showed no further interest in the planet once they had dispensed with the inhabitants. There was no occupation nor did they attempt to strip the planet of minerals. They simply took what they came for and moved on to the next one."

She nodded. "Yes, that's what I first assumed. The invaders had only come to those worlds to harvest."

The High Priestess had already known what he would find! The ramifications of this now began to sink in. His confirmation would be taken as a discovery if the Inquisition learned of this matter. Meaning the woman had just shifted all responsibility for this matter onto the Prime Chaplain's already over-burdened shoulders.

"What do you suggest we do?"

Her question took the Prime Chaplain totally by surprise. It was the same question that he was about to ask her. "We should be looking for the missing Imperial citizens," he answered. "As Prime Chaplain, that should be my only concern."

"No. Your only concern is to ensure the safety of your God-Emperor. Your idea is cowardly. It is a banal reaction to this dire situation. I did not drop the future of our great Empire into your fumbling hands only for you to hide beneath your robe."

The Inquisition were already on their way to his sanctum. He did not need to read her savage posture to understand he would not see another dawn. He looked away from her steady gaze. The Prime Chaplain climbed back into his chair. He no longer felt the need to show his respect to the woman as very soon he would soon be joining the minor heretic in his cell. The image of the second human world visited by the orbs was still showing on his monitor. It had been this incident that had put ex-Trooper Cole into that cell. He heard the man had fallen to his knees in the middle of a crowded spaceport and announced to all the startled travellers that the aliens were coming.

Philip took his eyes off the image. He turned to the High Priestess and offered her a beaming smile of his own, taking some satisfaction at seeing her posture soften. "Yes, of course. The priority should be to seek, locate, and destroy the aggressors. Therefore, I request that the minor heretic be pardoned. Restored to active service but under my protection."

That irritating head shake stopped him in his tracks before the Prime Chaplain could finish his proposal.

"The prisoner is a minor heretic. It is written in scripture the God-Emperor only considers the Imperial warriors worthy to wield his gifts. As you have been given holy dispensation, your blasphemy will go unpunished."

"Then what am I supposed to do about this fucking disaster when you force me to think along such narrow perimeters!" he cried. Immediately, he regretted the outburst. Holy dispensation did not protect him from committing the sin of dishonour to his High Priestess.

"The perimeters are just a fiction build across your mind, my friend. As Prime Chaplain, it is your duty to embrace the God-Emperor's holy judgement. Use what has been given to you, Philip. The answers you seek are within your grasp."

The Prime Chaplain stared at the other image of the Gizanti male cowering under the living vehicle and realised exactly what she was trying to say to him. "I use my special dispensation to order the minor heretic's execution to be postponed under this crisis is over."

"That is agreeable. Do you have any more requests?"

He nodded. "Yes. If it pleases the High Priestess, I would ask for authorisation for myself and the minor heretic to travel to the Gizanti home-world."

"And how do you propose to do that considering the restrictions imposed on the prisoner?"

"We still have the Gizanti prisoner and we still possess his ship. There is nothing within doctrine which prohibits humans from utilising alien equipment." The Prime Chaplain would still need to take his Index on his journey, but he decided not to mention that.

"Then it is decided." The hologram nodded to someone off screen before turning her attention once more to Philip. "You are to leave immediately. There will be a small squadron of Imperial marines which will serve as your protection. May the God-Emperor give you the will and determination to cleanse the alien."

The papal key was pushed out of the slot at the same time as the doors to his chamber slid open. Eight Imperial marines stood to attention before performing the same bow which he gave to the High Priestess. The Prime Chaplain used the moment to snatch the Index from her pale green holder and stuff the six-inch yellow crystal inside his robe.

"Sir, we pledge allegiance to you and to the God-Emperor's holy mission. We shall be your shield, your fist, and your council."

He gave them the appropriate response and bowed his own head as a mark of respect.

"If you would like to follow us, sir, we will take you to your ship."

Did they know exactly what kind of ship the marines were about to board? It would make an interesting observation if they had not been told beforehand. Most humans, including the military, had a deep mistrust of anything alien. To travel upon through space on a vessel which was allegedly alive would make even the stoutest of individual feel most nauseous. Come to think of it, how was the heretic going to react to this? From his observations, the human was not the most stable of individuals.

The Prime Chaplain composed himself and walked out of his room, wondering if he would ever see this place again. A part of him found this very exciting. It was the same aspect which understood that she had played him like an ancient piano. If he hadn't started to think around corners, these eight marines would have led him in the opposite direction towards one of the many execution squares in the city.

Everything had obviously been prepared even before the High Priestess had asked him to study the recordings. If the Prime Chaplain had not jumped through all the hoops, then that woman had many more subjects she could 'ask.'

He decided that it would be good for him to escape from the danger of court life for a brief moment in his life. Engaging an unknown highly advanced alien species would be far safer than dodging the drama encountered within this building every day.

# CHAPTER FOUR

After twelve service years, Trooper Cole believed that cutting through the black-weave, even in a vessel which bordered on the obscene, would be such a non-event event. He hadn't given it a moment's thought. Why should he? His mind was still reeling from finding himself on a Gizanti warship, crewed by humans and with some scary-looking Chaplain who all looked as confused about this whole situation as each other. Cole did his best to emulate their emotion. Despite his voice of reason explaining exactly why they had removed him from that comfortable cell and placed him on this alien vessel, he still had trouble believing Mr. Smith's words. So he was a prophet now? According to Mr. Smith, he had seen exactly what happened on this dirt-ball planet.

After spending his adult life crewing every class of ship in the Imperial fleet, Trooper Cole hadn't even considered that cutting through the black-weave would affect him, even on this *thing*. A living starship, something which looked like it had been ejected from the anal vent of a giant killcluster lizard. Every moveable part inside it bordered on the obscene. To make matters worse, if it could have gotten any worse, the interior looked wet. He had even tried to spend some of his time walking through this vile-looking ship with his eyes closed.

Trooper Cole lifted his aching head off the soft mud. The others were already inside the complex, leaving him and the Gizanti to act as lookouts. What a joke that was. Despite being far better trained than any of those marines, they all treated him like something they'd scraped off their boot. Those chapel-house-trained morons treated the Gizanti was more respect. It is almost as if none of the slug-brained fools realised that he was supposed to be their most valuable cargo.

He groaned while he pulled his body through this vile grey slime another inch. The Gizanti beside him moved up too. Unlike him, the alien moved through the muck like a pole sliding through grease. Not one particle of the planet's surface adhered to its soft underside or its armoured plating. How did it do that? Trooper Cole also noted that the Gizanti had altered its colouring to match the mud. He had no idea that the aliens possessed chameleon-like properties.

Perhaps if he wasn't alone, cold, and feeling like a building had fallen on his head, Trooper Cole might have been able to appreciate that perhaps he should have had a little more faith in Mr. Smith. He wasn't pardoned. The scary-looking Chaplain had made that fact abundantly clear, but he was out of that cell and still alive. That had to account for something.

"I almost wish I was back on the ship," he whispered. Trooper Cole glanced across at his Gizanti friend. "It might look like the inside of my guts, but at least it is warm." He sure hoped his voice of reason was okay. The marines refused permission to allow him to bring Mr. Smith. The Prime Chaplain did promise to look after Mr. Smith, but he said the words in such a way that intoned the scary-looking man would empty the contents of the small box down the toilet as soon as Trooper Cole left the ship.

"Human Cole. It is not proper to disrespect any Battle Sister in the presence of a Gizanti warrior." He turned on his side. "She has not yet adapted to these terrifying new circumstances. I am not confident that she ever will."

"Apologies. I do not always consider the possible outcome before opening my big mouth."

The Gizanti gave the approximation of a shrug. "You are only a human and do not understand our ways. No reason for you to repent. There is scope for enlightenment within your feeble mind; therefore, you and I can stay bonded." The Gizanti sat up and picked a bright red globe from what looked like a tree and popped it into his mouth. "The other humans who have tethered and defiled the Battle Sister do not have this honour." He then spat a wrinkled brown pip into the palm of his hand then offered it to Trooper Cole. "Take it and chew."

"You're kidding, right? I mean, it's been in your mouth."

"Would you prefer to continue feeling the effects from the weave-cut?"

The marines and the Prime Chaplain were all given a solution of chemicals to drink once the ship had emerged into normal space. As minor heretic, and because the chemicals were of Imperial manufacture, Trooper Cole didn't receive anything to nullify the adverse effects from the weave-cut. The marines found his suffering amusing. Just as they also applauded the Prime Chaplain's decision not to supply Imperial-made armour to him.

Trooper Cole squinted at the dubious-looking stone that the Gizanti had just dropped into his palm before giving the alien one last look before he opened his mouth and placed it on his tongue. He figured that the worst thing that could happen, the absolute worst, was he either be poisoned or he would choke to death. He swallowed the seed pod, figuring if it did kill him, it would at least save him from watching those moronic black-clad, dim-brained fools from shooting him.

"Thank you, Gizanti."

"You may call me Cladinus, human. As we are bonded, it is only proper we address each other in the correct manner."

"Fair enough. My name is Danny."

"I already know your name, Danny."

He now found he could lift his head without a rock avalanche crashing down over his ears. "Oh, that's better!" Danny followed the alien's gaze past the edge of this strange forest and over to the only artificial building in the vicinity. The complex clearly wasn't a Gizanti-grown building and, according to his new friend, it couldn't have been there at all. Cladinus told the Prime Chaplain, Danny, and the marines, before they landed the ship that the area around the new building was sacred ground.

Trooper Cole then returned his gaze to the alien. After spending most of the journey here locked in the same compartment with Cladinus, he believed he was beginning to recognise his facial expressions. Right now, it looked like he was laughing.

"Do you welcome death, human?"

"I have faced the bastard on too many occasions to be able to answer that truthfully." He turned his head and looked past the forest to where Cladinus had told the marine crew to land the ship. The alien was quite specific on where to land the ship. On this rare occasion, the dim-brained maniacs had obeyed him.

In spite of their utter self-belief that the human species was superior in every aspect to some dirty alien and their surety of having complete control over this Gizanti warship, there had to be a small part of their soul that still thought an unknown section of this living beast could still spring out from nowhere and eat them. At least, that's what Trooper Cole hoped. He also hoped that his Gizanti pal would be to wrestle control from the marines wherever he chose to, just in case they did decide to carry out that execution.

"Come on, Cladinus, are you going to tell me why you just asked me that question or are you just going to sit there, giggling away?"

The big alien sprang to his feet. He placed his huge hands on Danny's side, picked him off the ground, and pulled him right up to his face. "Death is the only certainty. We endure through our limited existence, hoping that the Nine Gods will reward our spirit after it leaves the body."

"You're hurting me," he said through gritted teeth. The alien didn't seem to hear him.

"We fill our world with life to appease all Gods but one. For Danak is the keeper of our bodies and to grow life from death will only insult him." Cladinus carefully turned and lowered Danny to the ground. "If the humans had taken the Battle Sister to a human planet, I believe you would see similar structures inside your burial grounds. Do you understand this?"

Danny rubbed his side. "Not a bit of it."

The alien pushed him backwards. "You need to go, Danny. Get to the ship before it is too late. Do not worry. I will attempt to stop them from reaching you. It is the least I can do for my bonded human."

"Wait, what are you talking about?" Cladinus had not stopped laughing. Danny was now beginning to wonder if he had read the alien's expression correctly.

"I do welcome death. I shall leave this world to the children we have grown and join my brothers and sister who now reside with Eight of our Nine Gods." He leaned closer. "Go, human. Do not allow our Ninth God to taste any more human flesh."

Danny stayed exactly where he was, despite the fact that he could now hear ominous rumblings coming from somewhere beneath his feet. "Start making sense, Cladinus. Remember, I'm not all that intelligent." He wished Mr. Smith was here. His voice of reason would know exactly what this weird alien was babbling on about. He shifted from leg to leg when the rumbling increased. The grey slop around his feet started to bubble up.

The alien reached for him. This time, Danny danced out of the way. "Oh no, big guy. You are not carrying me anywhere."

"Foolish human," said the alien, running straight at Danny. Cladinus grabbed his wrist and dragged Danny through the forest.

He had no chance of removing the alien's thick digits off his flesh. All he could do was to try not to slip while the Gizanti propelled him through the strange forest while doing his best to avoid the winding branches, which seemed determined to snag him and rip off what little clothing he still possessed. It was only when the ship came into view when the alien finally slowed down and stopped.

"Now go, human. Rejoin your race while you can still do so. Do not worry. The Battle Sister will take you home before she returns."

Danny's harsh reply died on his tongue when he turned and yelped at the sight of movement within the forest. It honestly looked like the wet, grey, sticky mess was coming alive. "What is going on, Cladinus?" He reached for his gun, realising at the last moment that he didn't have one. The bastards wouldn't even give him a knife.

"It is interesting to discover the shells or my brethren are still able to blend even though their spirits are long gone." The alien lowered his head. "No more warnings. Go now and let me return to the soil."

Trooper Cole then understood exactly what he was seeing within the darkness of the forest when the foul stench of death smacked him in the face. He reached up and snatched the alien's huge knife from the scabbard and ran towards the first tree. "Fine, kill yourself, do whatever you want. I'm not leaving them behind."

The alien charged at Danny and managed to grab him despite Danny dropping to the ground. "They have defiled the Battle Sister," he said after pulling Trooper Cole close to his face. "They have treated you like a worm. They deserve to die."

He could now hear them pulling their huge bodies through the thick mud. They were coming straight for them. Danny managed to gaze down the alien's thick body, his gaze stopping at the Gizanti's side arm. He doubted that even that would be able to stop these dead things. How can you even kill something that's already dead?

"Help them because I am asking you! They can't help what they are, just like those things behind us can't help what they are!"

"I cannot, Danny. Most of my species are now gone. I can no longer hear their voices. We number just a handful. Only the wanderers and the expelled insane remain. Let me die as I choose."

Trooper Cole lifted the heavy knife and placed the cutting edge against his own throat. "I do know some elements of your culture, Cladinus. If I die in your charge, No God will accept you, not even the Ninth." He pressed the blade deeper, feeling the razor edge break skin. Strange how he felt no discomfort.

Their shadows separated from the edge of the forest. In another couple of moments, it wouldn't matter about not worrying how deep he would have to push in this blade without seeking medical help. Cladinus leaned towards him then gently gripped the blade with his mandibles and pulled it away from his flesh.

"You confuse me so much," he said, after releasing the knife. The alien dropped the human before pulling out his blaster. "Perhaps one day, I might hear your voice, Danny." Cladinus pulled out his blaster and shot the closest figure, its armour-plating literally exploded, covering the trees behind it with shards of smouldering shell and lumps of boiling putrefying meat.

In the distance, Danny heard gunshots. He'd recognise Imperial weapons fire anywhere, and he knew that none of the guns those marines carried were nowhere as powerful as whatever the fuck Cladinus had just used. He looked past the burning stump and saw the floor were packed with those things. He couldn't even count how many there were, all heading towards them. "Cladinus, can you take them all out?"

The alien nodded. "Yes…"

"Then do it, before they all die."

"If you insist."

The Gizanti's hand pressed in a small wet lump located on the top of the weapon, raised his hand then fired again. Danny slammed his hand over his face when the world turned an intense white. He only took his hand away when he felt the ground beneath him rumble. The alien grabbed his arm.

"We must hurry. The ground holds the ancestors from thousands of years past and our bodies do not break down as quickly as a human corpse."

His weapon had cleared a wide path all the way through the forest, melting both dead Gizanti and the trees. The energy stream had even turned the material in the wet floor, fused it into glass. Even as he watched, the undamaged aliens were starting to make their way towards their route to the structure.

Cladinus was already running along the fused pathway. Danny raced after him, acutely aware that he'd pressed that blade a little too hard against his neck. He had swapped the pain from the weave-cut to feeling as though his head was about to fall off his shoulders.

They were almost through the forest when one of the dead Gizanti threw itself directly in front of Danny. "Shoot it!" he cried. "Please melt the bastard." He stumbled back as the huge armour-plated killing machine scuttled straight for him. He held the knife tight, seriously considering to finish the job he had first started as it sure wasn't going to help him out of this. Danny shifted to the left and screamed when another Gizanti's thick grey arm snaked out from behind an undamaged tree and almost grabbed him.

He dropped onto the glass floor and rolled to the side before he scrambled to his feet and ran towards Cladinus only to find the dead Gizanti was now about to attack his alias friend, and yet he still wasn't raising the weapon. What was wrong with him? Did he still want to die?

Danny leapt onto its back and desperately tried to find something that didn't feel like it was made of thick steel. He held on with his feet and fingers while dodging the dead thing's arms.

"Count three plates down from the top of her head," shouted the Gizanti while he dodged the dead alien's snapping mandibles.

He did as instructed, trying not to look at the amount of blood he was dripping onto the creature's armoured back. Danny found the tight join between the plates and slammed the knife deep, crying out in shock and pain when the dead Gizanti's movements suddenly stopped. He slipped off and crashed onto the baked hard ground, only to see three more dead things reaching for his splayed body. Cladinus scooped him up and ran towards the structure while holding Danny under his arm.

He set Trooper Cole down as soon as they reached the narrow doorway.

"I can't believe I left my knife stuck in that dead thing," he muttered, while peering into inside the building. He ran his hand down the surface. It looked like ordinary stone, and yet it was warm to the touch and felt very similar to the dead thing's carapace. Danny shuddered, deciding not to pursue that line of inquiry. There was enough light to see that the first chamber was empty.

Danny looked for anything else that he'd be able to use to defend himself and settled for a hand-sized rock close to his feet. It felt ridiculous walking into an area of extreme danger armed with something so primitive, but he had no other choice. After watching the big alien, it was obvious that his gun would be of no further use.

The Gizanti pushed him inside before he followed Danny in. "Cladinus, why didn't you fire? You could have turned that thing into a puddle of goo with one trigger squeeze."

"I regret that I could not, human. You did not allow me time to finish speaking." The alien moved out of the way. "They will not follow us in here."

The huge dead aliens were congregating outside the structure. They skittered between the alien trees and joined their companions on the path of grey glass. Further out, Trooper Cole groaned at the sight of more of them pushing their huge bodies out of the wet mud. "We're not going to get out of here."

The alien gently pulled him away from the doorway. "We should find the other humans. That is why we are here."

Danny pulled away from Cladinus. He ran back over to the doorway. "No, not yet," he said, trying to keep his emotions from boiling over. "Not until you tell me why those dead things will not come in here or why you refused to shoot that one." He spun around. "Tell me what the hell is going on here, because you do know. I'm not that stupid." Trooper Cole wanted Mr. Smith now more than anything else. His voice of reason would have known exactly what was going on here. Maybe he should have done exactly what the alien had told him to do in the first place. He had no loyalty to their unit, and despite the Chaplain's insistence that he was valuable cargo, Danny didn't think any of those black-clad idiots would risk their neck to rescue him.

"Because I was told," he replied, before turning around and shuffling towards another open doorway on the other side of the dim chamber.

"I'm so glad we had this conversation," he muttered, looking at his rock. "I feel so much better knowing all the answers." Danny had no other choice but to follow the large alien and hope that the reason the dead Gizanti stayed out there was not because of a larger, more deadly menace lurking in here.

Danny reached the other doorway. Cladinus had already entered so there was little point in being stealthy. Still, he kept his back against the wall and peered around the edge of the door just to be sure.

"This is unbelievable!" Millions of glowing icons covered every inch of the four walls. Danny ignored any potential danger and practically glided into the middle of the room, utterly engrossed by the alien symbols surrounding his body. A low hum reverberated from every icon. The uniform noise then separated into separate voices. He wanted to close his eyes knowing that without the distraction of the icons, those voices would become clear, yet Danny dare not separate himself from this reality. He would not be able to find his way back. He was vaguely aware of the Gizanti and another figure close by, but none of that mattered. All he wanted to do was to listen to the voices of the angels.

Another voice, with a deeper tone, started to take away the angels one by one. They retreated, slipping out of the choir inside his head. He mourned their loss, urging them to return, to stop merging with the symbols, but none took heed. Danny found himself kneeling on the stone floor, weeping into his hands while that one voice remained, telling Trooper Cole to stand up and face the first demon.

"Leave me alone!" he shouted back, but the voice obviously had no intention of listening to his order. Instead, it increased in volume, turning from coaxing into orders of its own, each one growing more urgent.

Trooper Cole slowly removed his hands away from his face when another sense kicked it. This one would not be silenced by his voice. The stink of dead meat now filled his nose. He felt something pawing at the tattered clothing on his back accompanied with harsh groaning and what sounded like the snapping of jaws.

"Move away from it now, human!"

Danny viciously kicked out, feeling the sole of his boot connect with something soft before he scrambled forward, not stopping until he reached a wall. The fact that the symbols were no longer glowing hardly registered as his brain was too busy trying to soak in the sight of one of the marines shuffling towards him. It hadn't occurred to the soldier that having a hole in the chest that you could push your head through meant that you should be dead.

Danny did the only thing he could. As the dead soldier lunged towards him, he stepped to the side and slammed the rock down on the man's crown. The blow seemed to have little effect, so he hit it again and again, not even stopping when the sound of his skull splintering echoed around the chamber. Trooper Cole only ceased his activities when the alien lifted his blood-soaked wrists up and opened his fingers. Danny listened to the rock hitting the floor while watching a single gleam icon on the far wall light up for a moment before joining the others and going dark.

"You might need this," said Cladinus, passing Danny the dead soldier's weapon. "I would ask you to clean your hands as well, human. His body fluid does not belong on you."

Trooper Cole crouched between the fallen rock and the twice-dead soldier and wiped the blood and mashed brain off his skin. "I'm sorry about this. You was not the most pleasant individual, but even you did not deserve a death like this." He looked up at the alien. "Are you ready to tell me just what the fuck is going on now?"

"We were once blood-thirsty barbarians like you humans, many generations before your species reached your only moon. Our empire relied on artefacts, tools, and buildings built instead of grown." He stepped back and traced the designs on the surface with one of his claws. "We did not construct this vile machine, but it is of Gizanti design. It is a resurrection chamber. When we invaded the worlds of our enemies, these were dropped from orbit onto their population centres. As you could imagine, the terror caused by the actions of these machines caused enough mayhem for our troops to take over and occupy a world with minimum casualties."

Danny shuddered to think how this dirty technology would be used if the Empire ever found out about it. He then tried to imagine just how great this Empire that had turned him into the lowest of the low would have coped if these aliens were still as warlike as Cladinus suggested. They wouldn't have stood a chance. Trooper Cole now understood the position they were really in. The Empire had come up against an alien civilisation more advanced than them. "I hope you don't tell anybody else about these things, Cladinus."

"We are bonded now, Danny. I have no secrets from you. Although I still wish you had gone back to the ship and allowed me to make my way to the Eight Gods." He finally took his claws away from the symbols on the wall. "It is difficult being the only member on my species walking upon the earth of the home-world. This is also why I can no longer use this." The Gizanti patted his sidearm. "It is our life-force which supplies the weapon's power. Every time it is used, we all lose a few seconds of life, as I am the only one left."

Danny nodded. "Right, it would drain you like a vampire. Wait, I thought you wanted to die?"

"The weapon does not know that." He turned. "Come, we had better go find the others."

He followed the alien out of this strange chamber. He tried not to think about why it had affected him like it did. Danny wasn't too keen on working out how they would leave this place either. The marines were armed, but none of them had anything able to create so much destruction with a single blast.

Imperial weaponry was supposed to be the most advanced in the known galaxy, although after witnessing the Gizanti's blaster, Danny was quite prepared to dispute that claim. Even so, they did possess energy weapons that would create an effect close to what he had just witnessed. Only, none of this unit had anything like that. The elite regiments always received the most advanced and up-to-date ordinance, while the rest of the regiments were issued with more basic variants.

He looked at this piece of junk. Up to now, Trooper Cole had not really studied the weapons held by this unit of marines. Until now, he had only seen the muzzle when they pointed it at his head. It was quite clear that these idiots were not as important as they made out, not if the only weapon the units carried were obsolete SS50s. These things were so old; they had even been modified for civilian use.

"The other humans are close by. Perhaps two levels below. Come. We must hurry. Time is no longer on our side."

Having said his piece, the alien scuttled away, moving a lot faster than Danny thought possible. He had to sprint in order to catch up to the Gizanti. "Wait, how do you know where they are? I cannot hear anything." That wasn't quite true. Danny could hear his own hard breathing as he attempted to keep up with Cladinus. As Trooper Cole expected, the alien did not bother to expand on his words. The Gizanti was beginning to get as annoying as Mr. Smith.

They reached a flight of stone steps. The alien stepped to the side. "You must go down alone, human. I cannot continue. I will wait here until you return."

"And you are not going to tell my why?"

"You have your gun, and the location of the other human. Do you want me to hold your hand as well?"

For the moment, Danny almost believed that his voice of reason was stood behind the big alien. "No, you stay there. I can deal with them."

# CHAPTER FIVE

He dove through the roaring flames, wincing as it licked his soft down. His blistered paws slammed against the concrete floor. Walish Din rolled into a ball, gritting his teeth as the agony of the impact burst open some of the blisters. He felt blood and pus dripping down his arms as he jumped up. There was no time to inspect the damage, Walish Din had to get out of here, from the fire and from the perpetrators which raised his home to the ground.

Five orange dragons were still within the settlement, methodically investigating every structure still standing. They were seeking out survivors, the hardy and the strong who had managed to live through their first wave of slaughter. There was no respite for any of his fellow species. The alien fiends could instinctively home in on the last of the shivering Diannin, no matter how well they hid under planks of scorched wood and rubble. Walish Din heard every single scream of utter terror in his mind, seconds before the orange dragons incinerated another member of his species.

He raced out of the burning shed, coughing and weeping. Completely aware that he was now the single remaining member of his tribe still living. Walish Din was also aware that if he didn't find some way to avoid their internal radar, those bastards would never stop searching for him.

Walish Din ran through a field full of blade-corn. Thousands of tiny serrated barbs tore out his fur as he pushed his way through the head-high crop, but the young Diannin was in too much pain to notice: agony from the cuts, burns, and blisters he had accumulated while trying to save his tribe, and the deep ache in his heart from knowing that he had failed.

Those orange dragons had even torched his beloved herd of glikgliks.

He burst through the edge of the field and ran towards Claynon Forest, hoping he would be able to lose them inside the dense tree cover. The Diannin scrambled up a steep slope, not stopping until he reached the final ledge. Only then did Walish Din turn around. The orange dragons were leaving the settlement, heading out in the opposite direction and travelling in single file. He dropped to his knees then fell into the soft grass, thanking his now deceased shepherd companions for allowing their own glikgliks to devour the brittle pods which should have covered the surface.

It took the last of his will to pull his aching body away from the seductive embrace of this lush vegetation. He needed to sleep, to rest and heal, but if he stayed here, out in the open, vulnerable and unaware, Walish Din would be walking with his tribe, elders, and spawn donors through the Plains of Gopin when he opened his eyes.

To find himself reunited with his tribe and to be free of all this terrible pain, both mental and physical, sounded like such a good idea. Walish Din would not have to worry about anything that happened on this plain ever again.

He moaned quietly and felt the waves of shame wash over him. Every plain on every level of life and death should be nurtured and loved. He was not a glikglik or a human. Wishing to live upon the next plain was sinful.

Walish Din lifted his head and cried as he saw the last of the flames devour his settlement. The orange dragons were now out of sight; no doubt another tribe was about to get a visit from those hateful fiends. His youthful spirit wanted to run to the next settlement, to warn them of their impending doom, but he now knew that it would do no good. Their elders would not listen to a shepherd from a different tribe; if anything, they would simply chase him off their territory. After all, his own elder thought he had gone insane. They had simply laughed at him. He sighed, only stopping to cough.

Why did he have to possess The Touch? It had brought him nothing but misery, humiliation, and death. Walish Din was a nobody, a waste of skin and down, who would probably have to share a plot once he did get to the Plains of Gopin. Knowing his bad luck, they might not even grant him that.

Thanks to this unwanted curse, he saw them incinerating his spawn donors before they even reached his settlement. He just did not understand why none of them would listen to his warnings. Why did none of them believe him? It just did not make any sense. They knew he had this curse of foresight.

He turned his paws over. Most of the damage inflicted upon his flesh when that burning wooden post had dropped down was already beginning to heal. Only one large blister remained whole. Walish Din carefully popped the tight bubble before he wiped the clear fluid down the side of his leg. His species possessed an incredibly fast metabolism, meaning that when by the sun rose to kiss the twin moons, his body should be almost repaired. If the hunters in the forest did not eat him first.

Walish Din got back onto his feet and limped towards the edge of the dark forest. It came as a scant blessing to know that The Touch would give him plenty of advance warning of any attack from the woodland predators by making him watch as they tore him into pieces before consuming his warm flesh. There was also the worrying notion of being unable to stop the prophecy from coming true. Walish Din had not been able to stop the orange dragons from murdering everybody he knew.

The trees before him had been here since before the dawn of their culture. It was written that some ancient race of aliens had visited their planet with the intention of conquering their world, but the Gods had come down from the vast plains and taught these aggressors about the value of love for the land, about how life rewards life. Before leaving, to return to their home-world, they planted these trees, native to their world, as a gift of thanks.

As a shepherd, he had seen how packs of spine-raptors run down herds of wild glikgliks, catching the fouls and tearing them apart. It didn't look like life rewarding life from where he was standing. His spawn donors had once explained that the Gods only allowed the predators to take the slow and the weak. It enabled the glikglik herds to thrive because only the strongest were able to pass on their best bits of the species to their offspring.

Walish Din rested his head against the smooth, grey trunk. He looked away from the now smouldering remains of his settlement and watched two leathery night-gliders dance through the twisting branches, high above his head. He wasn't the strongest and he certainly wasn't the fastest Diannin. The only reason he had staved off death was this cursed touch.

It was also said that the tree-planters were large in stature with orange armour covering their bodies. Walish Din shook his head before following the old path that led through the thick forest. He needed to stop thinking about stupid fairy stories and try to figure out how he would travel to the capital and arrive before the orange dragons turned every member of his species into a lump of charcoal.

He walked under the thick interlacing canopy of twisted branches, crushing the grass pods and Fline bulbs beneath his feet. Their sweet perfume took away the memory of the burning houses and charred bodies that Walish Din ran through in order to get away from those monsters.

How could the Gods allow this travesty to continue? If they left the plains to teach those other alien aggressors the value of peace, then why are they not down here already, stopping this new batch of aliens from annihilating anything that moved? It sounded like a cruel thing to say, but Walish Din did not care about those other worlds. As far as he was concerned, he would not shed a tear if every world burned if he knew it would bring back is spawn donors and the elders.

Not that he had that many tears left in his body to shed. He stopped again, this time besides a fallen spinner tree. He guessed the Gods were in as much shock as him. They were probably very busy right now, getting every new spirit processed. It wasn't every day when an entire tribe suddenly appeared on the Plains.

"Would you really let all the other worlds burn?"

The young Diannin screamed before throwing his body behind the spinner tree. He thought he was alone in here! Why had he not sensed another Diannin? More to the point, why did this new voice sound so amused? This was not the occasion to be joyous about anything.

He raised his head above the rotting bark and scanned the immediate area. Apart from the two night-gliders who had stopped their dancing to stare at him, there was nobody there. Walish Din wondered if the stress had finally scrambled his mind. Perhaps he was going insane, or perhaps none of this had really happened. He idly plucked a grass pod and pushed his claw through the brown casing. Perhaps if he wished hard enough, then Walish Din would wake up and he would be back in his hammock with his annoying herd of glikgliks outside his tent.

"Perhaps if you stopped feeling sorry for yourself and got back on your feet, you'd be a little closer to meeting me."

Walish Din snapped his head to the side and found himself staring at a human female sitting on the end of the spinner tree. She too had the remains of a grass pod in between her slender pink fingers. "How did you sneak up on me?" The Diannin got back on his feet and did his best not to look so vulnerable. It wasn't helped by the human giggling when he lost his footing and almost fell back into the leaf litter.

"You are the one from my dream."

She nodded. "Well, kinda. She is still on the other planet, probably going through the same trauma as you." The female picked up another grass pod, flicked off the brittle head, and watched with interest as the pod wings opened up and carried the seeds up into the air. "They chose her planet for a birthing world as well. Still, it could have been a lot worse." She dropped the stem, jumped onto the tree, and walked along the top, using her arms as balance. "They could have marked her planet for extraction. It's what will happen to the rest of the occupied worlds in the section of the galaxy."

"I don't understand any of this."

"Of course you don't, silly. You're just a simple shepherd. Don't let it concern you. Look, Walish Din. By the way, has any girl said that you're really cute?" She giggled again. "Sorry, no idea where that came from. Anyway, it's like this. These weird aliens have just started their mating cycle. They scoop up whole populations and transfer them all to worlds where they think they'll be safe. You see, and this is the clever bit, the ones that are displaced are altered inside and become incubators of the alien babies." She jumped down and sat in front of him. "It's all really icky and gross. To stop anyone from messing about with their grand plan, they also choose a warrior species to guard over them. This time, they chose the Gizanti."

"I want you to leave now."

"I bet you do." She leaned over and grabbed a piece of the spinner tree's bark. "You know what they say about life rewarding life? Well, it's true. Take a look at this."

She pulled the bark up revealing the rotten insides. Instead of seeing decomposing wood, Walish Din saw thousands of pale worm-like organisms running the length of the trunk. They all moved in one direction, towards her hand when she waved it up and down.

"The tendrils burrow up through the middle of the grass pod stem and deposit a seed of their own inside the pod. To stop the glikgliks from eating the pods, they secrete a foul-tasting gel which covers the top of the pod. Life rewarding life, you see? What you're involved in is no different, just a bit bigger, I guess."

Walish Din took one step back, wondering if he would be able to lose this human in the forest. He had gone mad and this was the proof. "You're not real," he said. "You can't be real."

The girl laughed. "Of course I'm not real, you silly little shepherd. I'm just another aspect of your fractured personality, with maybe just a touch of something else. If you want, you can call me Miss Smith, or The Voice of Reason. I'm fine though, I'll answer to both."

"Answer to both? What I want you to do is to go away! Just leave me alone!" he shouted, vaguely aware that his yelling had just frightened away the night-gliders. He had also just announced his presence to every hunter inside this forest. Walish Din spun around. No, he couldn't be blamed for that. If she hadn't shown up, he wouldn't have had to start shouting. The Diannin kept his back to her in the hope that she would take the hint and go back to wherever she came from. He no longer knew what he wanted anymore. In fact, the temptation to lie down right here and go to sleep so he could rest his aching mind and body sounded exactly what he should be doing right now.

Walish Din stayed still and made no sound, listening to the wind as it whistled through the branches. The distant roar from a large spine-raptor caused the returning night-gliders to fly off again. He could not hear the girl's irritating giggle, and that is all that concerned him. The Diannin turned back and smiled when he found he was alone again.

He walked back to the fallen spinner tree. The Diannin turned around intending to sit down when he changed his mind. The thought of all those vile worm-like things inside it made him feel sick. He did not want those things to sneak through the bark and start winding up around his body.

That spine-raptor took up the call again. This time another voice answered it, then another and another. Walish Din jumped onto the spinner tree, trying to work out where the hunters could be. They all howled as one, their combined voices chilled his blood. They were after him. He did not know where they were, although he guessed that they would be approaching him from all sides. It was how they hunted.

"Do you still want me gone, my little grass-eater?" the young human said with a smile. She had retaken her position, sitting on the edge of the fallen tree. "If I leave you again, you'll end up as dinner for your planet's equivalent to werewolves. You do know that there are some seriously fucked-up animals on this world." She raised her head. "Oh, there's one doggy." She raised her arm and waved.

Walish Din was beside himself with terror. Unlike the encounter at settlement, he could not escape from this one. He was dead.

The human girl then stood up, leaned over and pulled up the bark again. "Come on, in you get, grass-eater. The glikgliks hate the scent of these places and so do the spine-raptors."

That annoying smile dropped from the human's face when he refused to move, despite now being able to make out two shaggy heads poking out from between the trees.

"Get in here or die!" she yelled.

Walish Din whimpered, shuffling his feet through the leaf litter, heading towards those waving tendrils while the spine-raptors inched their way towards him.

# CHAPTER SIX

Trooper Cole made his way down the stone stairs, smiling to himself. This was almost like it was before the outburst, before he saw the Empire's true colours, before the appearance of Mr. Smith. It was difficult to remember what his existence was like before he walked into his life. Looking back, Trooper Cole should not even be alive considering the huge amount of stupid risks he had taken during his career.

He reached the bottom and followed the usual procedure in these circumstances. He might be on a rescue mission, but Danny had no idea of what danger the others could be facing, and after his encounter with the dead guy, he could not afford to take any chances.

That made him smile. Had his incarceration turned him into a more effective soldier? There was a big slice of irony right there. Danny altered the fire selector from safe to single shot then dropped into a crouching position before he slowly peered around the corner. He saw a short, wide corridor with three more open doorways, two on his side with the other one facing the other two. There was no cover available and he had no idea where the other units were. He turned and considered his options. Danny saw no other routes so logic suggested that the men would be in one of those three rooms.

His old self would have just walked straight into the first room, gun at the ready, and shot anything not in an Imperial uniform. Thankfully, he was not his self. There was also the factor that he wasn't in an Imperial uniform, so if any of those idiots were as reckless as he used to be, there would be a good chance that

Trooper Cole would end up like that poor bastard on the floor above him.

Danny got up and crept over to the foot of the stairs and picked up a handful of stones from the floor before returning to the spot by the corner of the wall. He rolled the smallest stone across the corridor floor and listened for anything that would give away their position. Sure enough, a hiss of whispered conversion reached his ear, followed by the noise of one of them getting up.

The marines weren't in any real danger down here, the cowards were hiding, cowering in one of the rooms. He glanced down at the antiquated weapon and understood why the Imperial armoury issued these guys with junk. They were not real soldiers, just jumped-up guards in a fancy uniform.

One of the remaining marines had left the safety of one of the rooms and was now walking towards the stairs. Danny sighed to himself. Their lack of professionalism proved he was right. Danny threw another stone, just to get the idiot's attention then waited. Sure enough, the marine waked straight past Danny's position.

"No words, no movement," he hissed, digging the gun's muzzle into the small of the marine's back. Danny leaned close to the man's ear. "You have not had such a great time here. Still, do not worry. I am here to save you from your shadows. Now, I want you to scream."

"You what?"

Trooper Cole jabbed the gun hard against the man's flesh, taking satisfaction at the quiet moan that left the marine's mouth. "A scream. Just remember that there is a minor heretic holding a gun on you. I am under sentence of death. There is no telling what I am capable of doing to you, young man." To reinforce the exaggerated stereotype, the guard's old drill sergeant and the chapel house priests would have told the young recruit, he leaned forward and gently placed the guard's ear between his teeth and bit down hard enough to break the skin.

The resulting scream was loud enough to cause Danny's own ears to protest at the sudden noise. He flipped the man around, fastened his hand over the marine's mouth, and flattened his back against the wall.

Like bumbling ducklings squeaking for their mother, the rest of the guards raced past him and their terrified man. To make his disgust of their behaviour complete, Danny saw that only one of them had brought a weapon. Trooper Cole silently waited for one of them to notice him before he slid the marine's knife from the man's scabbard and held it against his captive's neck. "Drop the gun." He glared at the squadron leader. "I want all of you to get onto the floor. With the exception of you."

If the hate Danny saw in that squadron leader's gaze was solid, he would be dead by now. "No more warnings. Do as you're told."

The squadron leader shook his head. "You are a minor heretic. It is forbidden for you to handle the revered weapons of our Glorious Empire. If you release our brother and gently place the weapon on the ground, your punishment will not be a danger to your life."

"You really did swallow the whole indoctrination rubbish. I am trying to save you all from a terrible death." He paused. "Okay, apart from this one." Danny applied a little more pressure on the blade, thankful that this knife didn't possess the same keen edge as the Gizanti knife. The marine in his grasp let out a little squeak. Danny almost pitied the coward. The marine honestly thought he was going to die. "You do know that I will kill him if you do not obey me."

The squadron leader shrugged. "His life is of little importance. We are but grains of sands upon the beach. The God-Emperor will tread upon our bodies, and we can only hope that we offer the soles of his feet a shared comfort."

Danny noticed the uncomfortable looks shared by the other soldiers. "You really believe the rubbish spouted from the mouth of those fools in our chapel houses who tried to fill our young heads with doctrine."

"If you continue to blaspheme, I will have no other choice but to terminate your worthless existence."

The marine holding the other gun took one step towards Danny. He was about to fire off a warning shot when the marine sighed heavily and placed his weapon on the second step.

"Pick that up, marine! I order you to kill the heretic."

The marine shook his head. "He is holding my friend. I cannot lose another friend today."

"You dare to defy a direct order?"

The squadron leader looked as though he was about to burst a blood vessel. "What happened on the level above?"

"Silence, heretic!" screamed the squadron leader.

"No. It is you who should cease talking," replied the now disarmed marine. "If it was not for your cowardice and incompetence, we would not be in this situation."

The squadron leader's hand reached for his sidearm, only for two others to grab the man's arms and pin him against the wall.

Danny released his captive. He guessed that the ongoing event would look more favourable if the marines could focus all of their grievances upon the marine now struggling to free himself while muttering words like termination, traitors, and mutiny under his breath.

"You left a brother up there!" said the disarmed marine. "He was dead yet still alive."

"He had become a deviant, possessed by alien demons."

"Then you should have shot him again and again until the soldier went up to the grounds of the fallen heroes, instead of running away." He looked over at Danny. "The heretic is correct. You are a coward."

"My name is Danny Cole," he replied, "and I am no heretic. As for the fate of your brother, he has now joined the fallen heroes." Danny was glad that Cladinus had advised him to wipe the dead man's blood from his skin. It would have been awkward to explain how their friend had finally died. He did not want the remaining troops to be alienated before he took charge. He walked over to the struggling man and slipped out the squadron leader's sidearm. "I had no idea these relics were still in service," he said. "Your band of under-equipped and poorly trained men do not deserve to be involved in a mission which will determine the very fate of our beloved Empire."

Those uncomfortable looks were exchanged one more time. These fools hadn't been told anything apart from that they were on prisoner escort. Danny passed the sidearm to one of the marines holding the squadron leader then walked over to the disarmed marine. "Pick up your weapon, soldier."

Trooper Cole pulled the weapon out of his hands and turned it upside down. "Another SS50. This one has very little charge. The lacarator is out of alignment, and your core is so brittle that in another couple more shots, the internals are likely to fuse." He pulled the soldier's emblem rank from his lapel, took out the clasp, and pushed the pointed end up through an aperture located behind the trigger guard. After a few more minor adjustments, Trooper Cole handed the weapon back to the soldier. "That should help. I have realigned the lacarator, tightened the bearings in the core cradle, and reversed the polarity in the neutron flow. Allow the flow to normalise and the charge should double."

"How did you do all of that?"

"What is your name, marine?"

"Magnus."

Danny shrugged. "Listen to me, Magnus. Loyalty to the Emperor will not always save your life in battle. That is the job of your equipment. Just as it is your job to ensure that your equipment is in fully working order. Although if you do not understand how your weapon operates, this function cannot be fulfilled. That is the job of your unit commander. Although, I doubt he will know anything but to spout hateful doctrine."

He stared at the other marines. "I would not look so pleased either. At least he brought his weapon. Oh, and your own prisoner has slipped out of your grasp."

Danny grinned at the sight of the enraged former squad leader as he wrenched the pistol from the marine's hand before pointing the business end straight at him. He did not look very happy. "I would advise you to turn around."

"Do not speak, you vile traitor!" he screamed. "On your knees and beg for your life. Show them the worm you really are."

"I really would advise you to look behind you." Trooper Cole began to approach the shaking man. He only paused when he thought he heard Mr. Smith's chuckling in his ear. His voice of reason would have loved to see this showdown. Once he returned to the ship, Danny would fill in the highlights of his little adventure. He might even embellish the part where he punched the ex-squad leader on the nose. That part hadn't happened yet, but it would soon be coming to fruition. The man squeezed the trigger. He then squeezed it again and again when nothing happened. Danny showed him the firing pin that he had pulled from the mechanism before handing the sidearm to the soldier. "A unit is only as good as the man who commands them. As I said, this man can do nothing but repeat scripture."

He snapped his fingers, wincing as the man screamed when the Gizanti grabbed him from behind. Danny had watched the alien's progress with interest from when he first emerged from one of the rooms, noting that none of the other units had given any indication that they were no longer alone down here. That alone gave Danny the confidence that this unit now belonged to him.

"How did you get down here, Cladinus?"

"The structure is of Gizanti design," he replied while dragging the struggling man over to the stairs. "I suggest we leave. The mission here has been accomplished."

Danny followed the alien back up the stairs, trying to figure out exactly what Cladinus had meant by that. As far as he was concerned, the mission had been to scout the surface of the Gizanti planet to look for clues as to where the aggressors could be heading next. Danny's mission was to sit around in the mud and act as lookout on a dead world while the squadron leader performed the important stuff. The man had told Danny this while smirking.

The man sure was not grinning now.

Unless Cladinus had made it his mission to ensure that Danny would take control of the squad. That would explain the alien's insistence of him going down here alone. If that was the case, how could he possibly engineer such a feat? Trooper Cole had not known this would happen until the opportunity presented itself.

Considering what he had recently discovered regarding the Gizanti species, Danny would not be all that surprised. Who knew what mystic powers these creatures could possess? The ability to foretell the future was fact. Was it not the God-Emperor himself who predicted the arrival of the new alien aggressor? Danny frowned at that thought, suddenly not wanting to give the concept any more consideration. He decided to just leave it at Cladinus just had the feeling that Trooper Cole would gain a squad and leave it at that.

The victory could be short lived though. Gaining command was the easy task. They still had to reach the ship, and he had not had the opportunity to watch them in combat, although his first impressions of their standard of training filled his heart with foreboding.

They reached the next level and entered the chamber filled with the symbols. Danny's gaze was drawn to the intricate designs, yet he knew the other humans would not be so fascinated by the icons covering the wall, not when one of their unit now lay on the floor with his head crushed and the object of the deed lying next to the body. He felt their unease deepen when the ex-leader of the men began to scream and thrash about, calling Cladinus an unclean, murdering alien.

Trooper Cole might have found the whole situation amusing if it hadn't been for the walls beginning to glow. This structure was feeding off the emotions rising from the soldiers. The more disquiet they make, the brighter the symbols glowed. Danny rushed over to the struggling man and slapped him across the face. The suddenness of the attack shocked him into silence. He stared at the men, holding their gazes. "It was I who did this. The man was already dead. His spirit is gone. This was just an empty shell." He run his fingers along the wall. "Accept this as truth." He looked over to Cladinus who promptly pushed the captive man's jaw shut before he carried him out of the room. Immediately, the icons dimmed. "Fear will be your greatest adversary. Remember this." Danny followed the alien out of the chamber.

"What would have happened just now?"

Danny looked straight at the soldier who had just spoken. It was the one who Trooper Cole had first caught. "Use your imagination," he replied, looking straight at the dead soldier. He turned around and walked out, not stopping until he reached the Gizanti. This was where their loyalty, bravery, and combat expertise would be tested. Danny had doubts whether any of them would pass this one. He looked out of the doorway, his heart sinking even further when he saw the dead aliens now carpeting the ground. Their grey, mound-like bodies stretched from the structure all the way up to their ship.

The alien dropped the ex-squad leader. "You are free to go, human. I shall no further bound you within my grasp."

The man went for his sidearm, obviously forgetting Danny now held it. He glared at mine. "That is mine. Give me it back."

Danny inserted the firing pin. "With pleasure." He gave him the pistol and stood back, watching the man struggle with his emotions. The ex-squad leader hadn't been prepared for Danny to hand it over so easily. "Are you going to kill me now?" he enquired.

"To give your new traitor unit the justification to assassinate me? I think not." He took one step out of the structure. "Although once the Prime Chaplain hears about this, you will all wish that I had granted you a quick death." Having said his piece, the man marched away from the structure.

"He's going to die out there."

"Yes, Danny," replied the Gizanti. "Perhaps I should have told him about the danger?"

"What do we do now?"

The ex-squad leader had come to a stop. He must have noticed the grey mounds now surrounding him. He spun around and raised his pistol, aiming it directly at the structure. The humans and the Gizanti dived away from the doorway as the man fired.

He did not get to fire again. The man's shrieks only lasted a few moments. Danny hurried over to the doorway and saw nothing but grey mounds of chitin armour shuffling against each other. There was no sign of the man. Danny did not mourn his death. After all, if events had travelled along a different path, it would have been the ex-squad leader ordering the men stationed around him to open fire. He did mourn the loss of that gun though. Their guns had enough charge for perhaps two to five shots each. Even if the SS50s could penetrate their armour and each shot was clean, they would still only be able to take out a quarter of them.

"What do we do now?"

Danny was about to propose that they climbed on top of the structure and see if they could make their way through the trees when the ship began to lift. He glared at Cladinus who kept his face perfectly still.

"The Battle Sister comes to us."

"How long have you two been talking to each other?"

"We have never stopped.

# CHAPTER SEVEN

It had not yet become the norm for the Prime Chaplain to brush over the more repulsive sections in the blasphemous construction, but he was becoming more at ease with the wetter areas inside the Gizanti spacecraft. He did not know whether this was a good idea as of yet. He stopped beside an Imperial-made viewscreen and watched the craft cut through the black for a few moments until the dimensional impossibly of the action caught up with his eyes and brain and made him go dizzy.

The ship was quiet. All the others were all stored in cryo-tubes. The Prime Chaplain had the adaptive treatment so he could stay awake during the journey. He walked through the quiet ship, trying to stay within the areas which better resembled the interior of an Imperial cruiser. Gizanti technology, if you could call it that, made him feel more nauseous than watching the ship travel through the territory belonging to the true Gods. It also made his stomach roll over.

He entered the main sleep station and stopped beside the alien. It truly was a fearsome-looking beast. Built for fighting and killing now thanks to the information he had learned from the many spy drones that he had sent with the expedition, the Prime Chaplain now knew more about the history of this enigmatic species that anybody else in the empire.

Even in deep sleep, the alien's outer shell had attempted to match the colour of the stark grey chamber. He brushed his long fingers across the dials that controlled the machine. With a single turn, the Prime Chaplain could end this animal's life. No amount of camouflage, armour-plating, or claws would help this creature.

His smile then froze in place when he began to shiver; the temperature had just dropped by at least ten degrees. The Prime Chaplain looked up towards what he assumed was one of the ship's monitors and smiled before moving his hand away from the controls. The temperature readjusted to a more comfortable level.

The Gizanti didn't need claws or camouflage. It appeared that the Prime Chaplain wasn't the only individual here who employed eyes to monitor the behaviour of their shipmates. He had known that the alien had somehow taken back control of the ship from the installed Imperial computer as soon as the craft suddenly lifted from the surface and floated over to the structure while finishing off what the Gizanti started by turning the surface beneath its hull into superheated slag.

What annoyed the Prime Chaplain more than the ease of which the alien took back what was rightfully his was that he had absolutely no idea that this craft possessed such a formidable weapon. He shuddered to think of the damage this craft could have caused on the Imperial planet. It had even flown directly over the Imperial Palace. Heads will roll over this; thankfully, he would not be in the firing line this time.

He walked passed the sleeping alien and stopped beside the first human. Nicolas Delaney, twenty-six years of age, had been indoctrinated into the chapel house guard at the usual age of twelve. His intelligence level was rated average. In his fourteen years of service, the soldier had not displayed any trait that would make him stand out from the other in his unit. He had no ambition to do anything but to continue existing. He was, in effect, the perfect recruit for the guard. Nicolas was the unfortunate individual who had allowed himself to be taken hostage. The ex-minor heretic, now this unit's squad leader, had surprised them all, especially the Prime Chaplain.

He walked past the other four sleeping chambers, each one occupied by other humans, each one fitting into the same chapel house guard template. The High Priestess had given him the most important mission in the history of the Empire and equipped this Prime Chaplain with a crew that wouldn't be trusted to complete a basic freight run without messing it up.

The Prime Chaplain stopped beside the remaining sleep chamber. This one should have contained the unit's squad leader.

Before the time of the Third Reformation during the first political purges, it had been the unit commanders who organised and led the initial round up of the priests of the false religions, the corrupt ministers of government, and the leaders of the multinational companies. Those early battles created many heroes and martyrs for the embryonic New Terran Empire.

Those fabled soldiers were the ones who showed the downtrodden masses the true word of the first God-Emperor. Those squad leaders helped to forge their new world and bring about a peace which has lasted for a thousand generations.

He looked down at the sleep chamber and sighed. When the Prime Chaplain was younger, he, like the others in his class, wished to become just like one of the legendary fighters told in the book of Genesis; it did not matter that their life threads were already spun. He was destined to serve out his life as a man of faith. Their ex-squad leader's life thread had been already spun as well. Unlike every other unit in the Empire, the chapel house guards were unable to rise to this revered position.

Perhaps that would explain why somebody had made a cloth effigy of the now dead man and stuffed it into the chamber. They had even stolen a melon from the food store and carved a crude face upon the surface.

When their new squad leader learns of their lack of respect for that position, Danny Cole might wish he retained his title as a minor heretic. He moved past the sleep chamber, deciding to leave the effigy alone. It will make a suitable warning for when Cole awakes.

"It has started, Prime Chaplain," said the Index.

He pulled the shard from beneath his cloak and raced towards the ship's bridge analogy. Philip was not sure if there would ever be another spike in Danny Cole's sleeping mind. He hoped there would be, for although they had learned so much from their visit to the Gizanti home-world, they still had no idea as to where or if the alien aggressors would target another planet.

"Are all the instruments recording to optimum capacity?"

"The system incompatibility has given rise to a number of communication issues. Consequently, the capacity is down to levels which makes replay ineffective."

Philip ground his teeth in fury. The alien ship still refused to grant full access to her systems to the Index, even for a moment. The bridge was now in sight, and although he desperately needed to get there, the Prime Chaplain slowed and stopped beside a Gizanti mind bridge. The crew used these devices to link with the ship during their own natural sleep periods. He also knew that they could be used by non-Gizanti races to directly talk to the ship.

Dare he use it, knowing just how much this ship disliked the Prime Chaplain? What other choice was there? Philip looked back at their sleeping alien and considered the option of waking him. He dare not. The transition to consciousness while still within the weave could cause the Tanzania's mind to collapse.

Having a seven-foot alien killer rampaging through this ship could cause more than a few complications. He tentatively pressed his index finger against the fleshy nodule by his chest and tried not to pull his arm away as twenty thick-ridged, bright-red pipes grew out from the wall around the nodule and slid along his flesh. He bit his bottom lip when the tips rose up an inch and blue needles burst through, growing towards his arm before they pushed through the skin.

His surroundings greyed out and he found himself back in his office on Earth. He blinked in confusion, wondering if he had just woken from a strange dream. It wasn't until he saw that his viewscreen now showed him lying on the deck of the spacecraft, drooling from the corner of his mouth when he remembered what he was supposed to be doing.

"I need your help."

His image on the monitor sat up. "Yes," said his image. "You do."

The image tried to smile. It looked grotesque.

"Please, I want you to allow the Index to reconfigure some of your systems. I promise..."

"No."

"I promise she will not linger."

"You are human. She is your slave. Humans cannot be trusted. You have no honour."

"This is vital! We need more power."

"No."

The Prime Chaplain stood up and walked over to the monitor. "Do you want to die? Do you wish the last known member of your species to die?"

"Cladinus is my friend, but he is not the last. I am friend to all Gizanti."

"Danny Cole is the friend of Cladinus."

"Danny Cole is a friend of my friend."

He wanted to smash his head into the viewscreen. Every second spent arguing with this childish life-form meant more potential data was lost. "Danny Cole might know where all your other friends have gone. Please help me to find them and all the other humans. Only you can help. Only you can help all your friends." He turned around and turned his back on the viewscreen. "Only you can be a hero."

The Prime Chaplain opened his eyes. He was still lying on the deck, but he was no longer attached to those pipes. Philip jumped to his feet and ran onto the deck. He carefully inserted the shard into the Imperial interface and impatiently waited for the shard and the interface to align.

"Status update, Index!" he shouted, as soon as the process was complete.

"All the instruments are recording to optimum capacity."

"Thank you, ship. Thank you!" He walked over to the sleeping man, stored in his very own sleep chamber, and leaned over the oblong casket. Trooper Cole had insisted on having that box placed on his chest before Philip put him to sleep. He fully understood the split caused when the seizures first took hold of Trooper Cole. It had been his mind's attempt to segregate the new ability, to contain it so it would not cause a total meltdown if there ever was a threatened melding of the two personalities.

"You have your very own Pandora's box, my friend," he murmured. "Index, transfer current activity to the forward monitor."

"She will not allow that."

The Prime Chaplain heard the words but refused to believe them. "Repeat your last statement, Index."

The Index did not reply. He wrapped his fingers around the shard and was ready to detach it from the interface when the forward monitors burst into life. "About time." Philip kept his hand in place as the screen only showed him static. "What is this?"

The picture cleared. It showed the interior of this ship with the focus on the Prime Chaplain's body as he laid on the deck. His eyes travelled down his doppelgänger's shaking form until he reached his right foot which was attached, via another ridged blue pipe to the floor. The Prime Chaplain jumped back in shock as a panel in the deck in from of him sank a couple of inches before it slid out of sight. He groaned as another thick pipe rose out of the hole.

"Danny Cole is suffering."

He pulled his gaze away from the deck and saw his doppelgänger was now sitting up.

"Friends help friends. Are you his friend?"

The screen split into two images. The one on the left still showed himself stroking his chin while the new image displayed what looked like some ancient battle. Hundreds of Imperial Mechs strode across some unfamiliar battle-damaged urban landscape. The Prime Chaplain frowned. That the landscape was not as unfamiliar as he first believed. Amongst the blasted ruins, Philip could make out the familiar sigil of the Terran Empire carved into a couple of the larger buildings in the distance.

He saw seven armoured soldiers run out from behind a collapsed wall. They all dropped on one knee and started to fire their weapons at the closest machine. "This cannot be real," he said. "It has to be fiction!"

The Empire had taken all of the mech battalions out of active service hundreds of years ago when a couple of the lesser races had begun to acquire more powerful energy weapons. Within several years, the new technology to the other races despite the Empire's attempt to punish any species who dared to defy them. The mechs were formidable weapons. The sight of a full complement of these huge metal monsters striding across the land was enough to destroy the moral of most alien species who refused to bow down to the God-Emperor. If the streak of stubbornness still flowed through their unclean bodies, then those mobile weapon platforms simply turned everything within sight into molten slag.

The balance of power changed when the alien races started to fight back using their stolen technology. The energy weapons sliced through mech armour like a hot knife through butter. With enough mobile units, the aliens were easily able to wipe out dozens of the advancing mechs before the pilots were even able to fire off a single shot.

The Empire used shield generators for their ships and larger models to protect their worlds, but the mechs were simply too small to warrant the use of such power hungry devices. It was far simpler to retire them all and to go back to using planetary bombardment followed by shock troops launched from orbit.

Those soldiers were using energy weapons against the advancing mechs. It didn't take the Prime Chaplain long to realise that those were Imperial energy weapons, light years more advanced than anything those blasphemous deviant aliens had used against these ancient walkers all those centuries ago.

They might as well have been throwing Trooper Cole's rock for all the effect they were having. The blasts slammed into an invisible dome around each advancing walker and dissipated across the barrier. Still, the soldiers continued to fire, standing their ground even though the mechs selected one marine at a time and vaporised them.

"Please tell me this isn't happening right now?" His other self just shrugged before going back to playing with his chin. Philip watched in horror as the mechs now moved closer to the largest ruined building before stopping. At this distance, he now noticed some distinct ambiguities on the surface of each machine. They were old Imperial mechs, he had no doubt of that. Unlike the ones he remembered from watching the history reels, these displayed distinctive embellishments across every machine. Someone or something had modified them. The Prime Chaplain then saw the ultimate irony in this lopsided battle.

The Empire was the blasphemous deviant alien, desperately defending their territory against a civilisation with a technology that was light years ahead of anything they possessed. All the mechs raised their primary weapons. The view shifted, panning across the blasted landscape, only stopping when the largest structure on the land came into view. "Oh no, how can this be happening?"

He stared in horror at the damaged Imperial Palace. That squadron of mechs had come here to rip out the Empire's beating heart and from what he had already observed, there was nothing anyone could do to stop this.

His other self tapped his finger on the other side of the monitor before pointing at the deck. The Prime Chaplain saw the two pipes beside his feet. He took a deep breath and nodded. "Fine, go ahead, do what you have to do."

He gently lowered his body, trying not to allow his fear consume him. The Chaplain did not want to do this, but what other choice did he have? He sat down then raised both legs. Swallowing hard when the two pipes lunged forward, their openings enlarging before sliding over his feet. The Prime Chaplain winched when the needles were pushed into his ankles. Philip's vision greyed out. He heard gunfire and shouting. He then heard somebody screaming, not realising that terrible sound was coming from him.

# CHAPTER EIGHT

A burly trader twice his age pushed passed him, his face crunching up in annoyance when Walish Din failed to move out of the trader's path fast enough. Just days ago, an incident like this would have played upon the shepherd's mind for hours.

He turned around and watched him make his way over to a stall selling local fruit. The trader hadn't stopped muttering under his breath. Walish Din broke into a grin. So many of his kind and none of them cared about the invasion happening on the other side of the valley. Such is the mentality of his species.

Walish Din moved out of the way of a woman carrying a basket laden with decorations carved from spinner tree wood before walking towards the fruit stall. He had never seen so many varieties of fruit in one place before.

"How your species has thrived is beyond me."

He wondered how long it would be before she turned up again. The human girl had saved his life, but that didn't mean he should talk back to her. Walish Din stood a little too close to a Diannin female, finding his feeling of belonging increase when she brushed past him. Unlike the trader, she didn't say anything. Not that this bothered him, he just wanted to feel her soft down against his. It had been a few hours since he had rolled out of his hiding place and rubbed his front and back across the dry leaves in a desperate attempt to banish the vile itch left from all those tendrils.

Some of that fruit sure did look tasty. He had forgotten when he last ate. The prices were reasonable too. Walish Din smiled at the burly trader who scowled back at him. The trader's expression soon altered when the shepherd pulled out a couple of coins.

"It's like that, is it? You're going to ignore me like you're ignoring the advancement of those soldiers? I'm not going away, and you can be sure as hell that those soldiers aren't suddenly going to turn around and go somewhere else."

As he had walked through the bustling market, he had done everything to avoid the crimson glow bursting across the horizon. Walish Din hadn't been the only one to avoid looking at the approaching storm. They were all very aware that it was likely their comfortable little lives were about to come crashing around them.

He bought two klinder globes and retired to a collection of swinger chairs on the edge of the market so he could devour his purchases. Disquiet and unease rippled from every Diannin in this market. His Touch amplified their emotions to a point where it was difficult to focus. Yet, their self-belief that those distant fires, explosions, and weapons fire would never reach them almost cancelled out their shared discomfort.

As he bit into the succulent fruit, he could hear the human girl still rattling on about how sentient being plant-eaters were all the same: more content with sticking their heads in the sand whenever anything threatened their existence. Walish Din couldn't argue with that. He had lived through the horror that was about to fall upon his kind and here he was, eating klinder globes, and enjoying in the general atmosphere of this market, basically acting as though he did not have a single care in the world.

"I have heard of some toxic plants which a selection of humans use to displace their notion of reality."

The girl chuckled. "Oh, so you've decided that I exist again. That's nice. I hope you realise just how much you hurt my feelings by ignoring me, Walish Din."

Her face distorted into a look which he translated as a pout; either that or she was about to have a fit. "Are you aware of what I speak?"

"Of course I am, I'm not a complete idiot. You're talking about drugs. Yeah, there's a few who defy Imperial doctrine and get wasted on occasion. What of it?"

"That is how I feel right now," he replied. "The proximity of so many of my kind is intoxicating, my pretend human companion.

All the others here draw from the energy given out by so many Diannin in one spot. I understand your derisive comments about our mentality and it is true." He took another bite of the fruit while watching that crimson horizon draw closer. "I am not sure why I am explaining this to you. If you are part of me, then you should already understand." Walish Din dropped the core into a bin and stood up.

"Because not all of me is from you, that's why, silly. Now, if you've finished stuffing your face, shall we continue on our journey? Time is pressing, and I really don't want you to get caught up in the stampede when those adapted Gizanti warriors get to the market."

"They're all going to die." Walish Din felt a brief moment of sadness spear through the haze of contentment. There was not a single thing he could do to prevent their slaughter. He had already tried the running around and gesticulating in front of his own tribe. All that succeeded in was from every one of them laughing at him. If he tried the same approach here, it is likely they would pelt him with rotten fruit. It did not matter about the terror on the horizon; he was not an elder, therefore, he did not have a voice. Walish Din looked around the market, taking in the sights and the smells. It felt right to remember this scene. What made this even more tragic was that the locals believed this area was sacred and protected by the Gods as this was the spot where they came down from the Plains of Gopin to change the ones destroying their subjects.

"Some of them will die," she replied, keeping her voice quiet. "The ones which do live through the next few hours will be in trauma for the rest of their short lives and that's a good thing." She took his arm and led the shepherd towards the wide gate which opened out into the main town.

The explosions were getting very close now. Some of the locals were now starting to glower at him, as if all this was all his fault. "How can it possibly be a good thing?" Walish Din reached the market gate. A particularly loud explosion emanating from inside the forest caused even the burly trader to jump.

"Because it will," she snapped. "Look, you really need to get a move on, Walish Din. This is where the soldiers are heading for?"

"The market?"

"No, the spaceport!" The human girl climbed onto the gate. "What will this lot do when they see your orange dragons? I bet they won't continue haggling over the price of those stupid klinder globes."

He hadn't thought about that. At the first sight of those monsters, they would all group up, to form a protective bunch, with the tribal elders in the centre. "We need to get out of here!" The outcasts, beggars, and strangers would be the last ones to join the group. It was them who would first feel the monster's blue fire engulf their bodies and that list included him. He would not be able to withstand the call of so many voices.

The Diannin jumped over the gate and hurried past the two-storey buildings that made up the settlement's commercial district. The narrow streets were largely empty. Most of the locals would be in the market today. He risked a glance over his shoulder, and wished he hadn't. The fires from the explosions and the weapons were tearing through the dense forest. He saw movement in there as well. At first, Walish Din thought it were the woodland creatures fleeing from danger, until he saw just how much destruction their progress caused.

The orange dragons were coming! He wasn't the only one to spot the movement either. A ripple of concern spread faster than the forest fire, causing the Diannin people to drop whatever they were doing and start to converge around the stone pillar in the middle of the market square. He felt the tug as well.

"Turn around, you idiot! Face me. Look into my pink hairless face. Come on, Walish Din, do as you're told. Fucking look at me!"

It took a great deal of effort not to run back down towards that gate and join his comrades. Their linked calling filled his head, almost drowning out the panicked shouts from his imaginary companion. Walish Din might have even ignored even her if that single orange dragon had not emerged from the edge of the flaming trees and fired his evil-looking weapon straight into the middle of the marketplace.

The blue fire incinerated every Diannin that had ran over to that stone pillar, including that burly trader. The signal just flew apart, freeing the shepherd from his mental bounds. He backed away, watching in utter horror as more orange dragons strode out from the burning forest and preceded to murder his species. None fired their weapons. They did not need to. The panicking Diannin people were running about in every direction. All the monsters had to do was wait until one of them smashed into their pelts before they grabbed the little creatures and pulled them apart.

"Come on, there's nothing you can do!"

He spun around and ran up the narrow street, feeling like the greatest coward in the universe. It didn't matter that he knew there had not been a single thing he could have done to alter what he had witnessed. If Walish Din lived past today, which he now doubted, those images of the aliens slaughtering his own kind and enjoying it would never leave him.

He slowed down then stopped and leaned against a stone wall while trying to catch his breath. There was more activity further up the street. It looked like some kind of festival going on. He moaned in horror at the inevitable fact that this mental torture was about to replay. There were almost as much Diannin people crowding the street as there was in the market.

"What am I going to do now?" He looked in both directions, looking for a side street that might take him around them, but he saw nothing that fitted that description. The orange dragons would soon be coming up here once they had killed everybody in that market. Walish Din turned around.

The aliens were already at the gate! Behind them, the shepherd saw that the orange dragons had not killed all of them. A couple of individuals had managed to hide under carts and market stalls. A young woman who looked about his age was pulling the broken body of an old Diannin down some stone steps. She then carefully leaned the body against another cart before she threw her arms around the body's neck and started to wail.

Two of the orange dragons turned their massive heads but, thankfully, none of them bothered to leave the gate in order to dispatch the female. Thanks to his curse, her misery became his misery, and Walish Din received the full brunt of her shattered emotions.

\*\*\*

Maufain Sil only came down here to make sure her grandfather had taken his medicine. The awkward old glikglik would not accept that he was not a young man anymore; always trying to prove to the other traders that he could keep up with them.

She hugged him tight and cried, not caring if the giant demons came back to kill her like they had with the others. Maufain Sil had just lost her only surviving family member. He had left her lying amongst all this death to join both her spawn donors on the Plains of Gopin. The female held onto her grandfather and quietly sobbed, not knowing what she was going to do now.

\*\*\*

"Walish Din, you need to move!"

He slowly nodded, while trying to pull The Touch from out of the female's mind. "She needs to get away from here."

"The girl is safe. It's you who needs to get out of here."

He turned back around and moved closer to that celebrating crowd, still unsure of how he could get past them.

"Life rewards life," said the human girl. "Isn't that one of your species favourite sayings?"

"I suppose. What of it?" Walish Din reached the perimeter of the crowd. He saw a narrow gap between two large Diannin men and attempted to push his way through the gap. Not for the first time in his short life, he wished he wasn't so slight. These two hadn't even noticed him trying to squeeze his way past their bulky bodies.

"It isn't enough to just exist, Walish Din. In order for life to reward life, you must embrace your time here, no matter how long that stay will be. None of your species live your lives to the full. You only embrace the comfortable repetition of routine and tradition. This is why most of your kind will not exist once the converted Gizanti have finished here."

"That's very comforting," he replied, still trying to find his way through this moving crowd. "I would be most thankful for a little help here instead of insulting every Diannin left alive."

"That girl will live through this purge, and so will a few others. Whether it is enough to ensure the continuation of your species rests upon your resolve to finish your journey, Walish Din. Embrace your life, you stupid shepherd. Make your mark, shout out your status, show this stupid flock of two-legged sheep that you are here!"

"I don't understand!" An old man had now got in his way, and no matter how hard he pushed, just like everyone else his age, the ancient Diannin would not listen to a word from anyone younger than him.

"The Gizanti approach, shepherd. In another few moments, the Diannin on the edge of the crowd will see that death is near."

Walish Din tilted his head back and screamed out. The old man jumped, but he still did not move. The young shepherd then did something that no young Diannin had ever done. He curled his fingers into a fist. The old Diannin's eyes widened. He must have realised Walish Din's intention and tried to move out of the way, but he was too slow to avoid the shepherd's punch.

He hit the old Diannin between the eyes. The blow knocked him back, tripping up over somebody's feet. The people around the old Diannin all moved apart in tandem as his body fell onto the cobbled stones. A shocked silence hovered over the crowd. Walish Din felt their eyes drill into his body. He had just committed the ultimate crime.

"Well, that's one way to shout your status, I guess." The human stepped over the groaning Diannin. "Hurry up, you've bought yourself another minute. Don't let it go to waste!"

The crowd parted as he walked towards them. He had never felt so much hatred directed at him. This was almost as bad as the misery Walish Din felt when he reached into that girl's head. He was now truly alone. No other Diannin would ever talk to him again.

"Stop it with the self-pity. If you don't get out of here, there won't be another Diannin left in the galaxy. Move your legs, it's not far now."

He moved past the remaining members of his species, seriously wondering if he would ever see any of his kind again. Walish Din heard their screams and began to sob. He would not turn around again though, not this time. As he knew that if he did that again, this shepherd would not be able to continue. He would die here.

"You're nearly there, there isn't that far to go now. Keep moving, you're doing great, far better than I thought you would. I…"

"Shut up, shut up, shut up!" he screamed. "You are making it sound like I have just participated in some stupid competition. My own kind are dying around me."

"Don't you think I don't bloody know that, you silly little shepherd? If it wasn't for my intervention, you would be able to stand there and have your little temper tantrum. I am the voice of reason, Walish Din. I can see that they're all dying. I have eyes you know." She stood directly in front of him and placed her hands on his shoulders. "The galaxy is indifferent to your suffering. It doesn't care about you or your species. I care about you, and I also care about the ultimate survival of your species."

"By letting those orange dragons murder them all? Get out of my way. You talk in riddles and contradictions." The girl refused to move. "Leave me alone. I no longer wish to look at your annoying hairless pink face anymore." If the orange dragons were coming up here to destroy the spaceport, then all he had to do was find another way down this hill. Perhaps he could look for the pretty young Diannin he saw in the market. Walish Din saw more sense in trying to help her get over her grief than to continue on this silly notion perpetrated by some imaginary companion.

The human girl had not moved. "No," she growled. "You ain't chickening out, not now, not after the trouble I've gone to get you here." Her fingers dug into muscles. "Your destiny is far greater than you could even imagine, you silly little shepherd. It isn't just your ridiculous species whose danger of extinction hangs in the balance. You need to forget about the girl in the market."

Walish Din felt water drip from his eyes. "What is this?"

"They are tears, shepherd."

"How? We do not leak water. I thought only humans did that."

The girl nodded. "You're crying, you idiot, because I'm crying. There are over twelve million displaced humans on your planet, Walish Din. They are all going to die a horrible death."

"I'm so sorry," he murmured.

The girl cast her gaze towards the village before turning her attention back to him. "I know you are, and that's why you have to continue." She shushed him before he could object. "Listen, listen to me. Those humans are living incubators. Growing inside their bodies are billions of spores, encased in several hard shells. Once the shells are ready, what's left of the human bodies will dissolve. Can you guess what will happen then?"

Walish Din shook his head.

"Those hard shells will appear over every planet, infested by humans, in the galactic expanse. They'll crack open and release their spores. Within a few days, there won't be a single human being left alive." The girl paused. "The human species will no longer exist, meaning that their continued oppression will be at an end."

Walish Din wasn't sure how to take this news. Everybody knew that the Terran Empire was at heart evil, but that didn't mean that the entire species should die. He could hear those orange dragons in the distance. Still, once those incubators were off his world, then surely the orange dragons would go as well, leaving them alone.

"Can you guess what will happen then?"

He was sure that she was about to tell him no matter how he replied.

"The Empire will find out where those human incubators originated. Before you could say glikglik, Imperial warships will fill your sky, and it will be the last sight you avert see before they open fire and burn this world."

Walish Din spun around and walked away from her, feeling sick.

"There's a chance you can save your planet and all the others," she shouted after him. "Stay here and you'll surely die."

He continued walking away, heading towards the largest building in the town. Walish Din heard the sounds of human and alien shouts coming from that building. He felt the tension mounting the closer he got to the spaceport. There was a chance that he could still end up dead before he even figured out how to get off his home-world.

This wasn't the first time he had been to this alien-looking building. When he was younger, his spawn donors brought him and the other yearlings to the market in order to enrich their teaching. Before returning, they brought them all up here, up to the spaceport, built by the humans. The sight of all those silver metal birds lifting off into the sky made some of the other yearlings cry out in terror. Walish Din saw the look of superiority on some of the human faces. They obviously thought it funny that their superior technology scared these primitive creatures.

The humans didn't look quite so superior now. Walish Din stopped a few metres from the grand archway. Several humans as well as a smattering of aliens bustled around the spaceport entrance. Right now, they all wore the same expression as his yearling friends. Walish Din gained no comfort from this.

He passed through the archway, aware that his imaginary human female had caught up with him. "Now what do I do?"

His voice of reason stayed silent.

"Come on, answer me." Walish Din dare not take another step towards that crowd of large, angry looking people. In fact, the urge to flee gripped him by the throat when he heard gunfire.

"Don't run!" she hissed. "Don't you dare leave here."

He had to jump out of the way when two more humans rushed past him and joined the rest of the humans. As they pushed their way closer towards the building, Walish Din saw the reason for the crowd's lack of movement.

There were three men blocking the small archway which led inside, each one dressed in black armour with accompanying black weapons held in their hands.

The panic-stricken men were not alone. Beside them, stood another, older man. He too was dressed in a similar uniform, but unlike the others, the armour hung off him. It looked as though a child was wearing it. This didn't seem to bother the older man one bit. Unlike the jittery security personnel, he carried on doing his job like he had all the time in the world, much to the annoyance of the waiting crowd who, by the looks of it, were becoming more uneasy by the second. He took a ticket out of a crying man's hand, fed it through a grey, rectangular device in his hand, then studied the readout for what seemed like an age before nodding three times. Two of the security then grabbed the crying man and literally launched him into the building.

More humans pushed past Walish.

"Look at the old bastard's face; he's loving this," cried the girl. "I bet it's the first time in his life when he's actually felt like someone important."

Some of the humans were now throwing credit chips at the guards and pleading to let them pass. This was going to get ugly real soon. He felt the tension in the air. It made the urge to run even more intense.

Two shots fired from inside that crowd, followed by a dozen more shots. They came from beyond the spaceport. Walish groaned loudly when he saw gouts of flame shoot into the air, further down the hill. The orange dragons had entered the settlement!

"Stay with me, Walish Din. Don't you dare run now!"

The security guards now fired into the crowd. Three humans fell to the floor. Thick blood pooled out from under their stomachs. Half the crowd turned and ran while the remaining humans dropped to the floor. Screams of mercy and crying battered his ears, yet above the noise, Walish Din still heard his voice of reason telling him to run. To run towards the three guards.

Every cell in his body howled in protest as he turned to face the human security guard. Walish swallowed hard then ran straight at them, expecting to be cut down at any second.

"Believe in The Touch, it will protect you. It will always protect you."

Her calming voice did help to smooth away some of the terror, but it didn't stop him from jumping out of his skin and biting his lip when one of the guards reached forward and slapped his large hand on the Diannin's shoulder.

"Come on, sir, let's get you on the shuttle."

The man pulled him inside and physically propelled him over to the waiting doors. The shrieks of the humans he'd left behind filled his ears, along with the sickening sound of weapon's fire coming from the humans and from the orange dragons.

The girl had been right. They were heading towards this spaceport. He reached the door just as the orange dragons slaughtered the last of the humans by the entrance and pushed their huge bodies through the narrow gap.

Walish Din's last view of the spaceport before the hatch softly closed was of one of the orange dragons stamping on that ticket inspector while blindly firing its energy staff into the air.

Somebody gently picked his shivering body off the soft carpet. He turned his head to find an older human with a shock of grey hair trying to escape out of a black-peaked cap looking down at him. His large green eyes were full of concern.

"This is the captain, Walish Din. Tell him to alter his course. Tell him that he has to take you to Altus Gamma."

Walish Din blinked, before relaying the message.

"But, sir, this is a passenger liner. We can't fly into another war zone. I'm not even sure that we'll escape from this one."

"Ask him again."

Walish did as his voice of reason commanded. The captain of the liner released a tiny sob before finally nodding. "Yes, right away, sir."

The girl kneeled beside the young Diannin. "You need to prepare yourself. What you've just undergone is nothing compared to the challenges which you're about to face.

# CHAPTER NINE

He opened both eyes, vaguely aware that the most important thought in his life was slipping through his barely coherent mind. Danny Cole blinked rapidly, trying to hold onto the last few fragments of whatever had been running through his dreaming mind.

The last fragments of whatever he'd been thinking about abruptly vanished when the IV line attached to his arm pumped his body with a cocktail of drugs designed to bring both his mind and body out of sleep suspension. Danny sighed heavily before looking around the room. He expected to see the others in the same situation as himself. All groaning, trying to move with each one wearing a vacant expression.

Danny frowned. He was the only one awake. The others were still inside their suspension pods. The recuperation procedure hadn't started on any of them. He slowly sat up, wondering if something had gone wrong.

"Sleep well?"

Danny sat up. His box fell onto the floor and the dried moss rolled out and vanished down a small hole next to another sleep-pod. "What the hell?" He groaned at the sight of his so-called voice of reason sitting at the edge of his sleep pod. So much for being alone.

"Oh, don't worry about that anymore, Danny. I think you've come far enough to dispense with the totem."

"What?"

"The box, Danny Cole. It's just a simulacrum, a focal point to enable your waking mind to deal with your special status."

He shook his head, hoping the apparition would leave him alone.

"You didn't check in the corner of your bed."

Danny glared at Mr. Smith. "Why are you here?"

"That's the important thought, Danny." The apparition grinned. "You were thinking about the time when those bastards had incarcerated you, remember? Well, during your mad stage, when you were trying to make an image of me by collecting moss. There, now that that's out of the way, let us get you back to a more important subject. Namely why you're awake while the others are still sleeping."

"Go away!" he spat. "Go on, get out of here, and don't come back."

"Oh, don't be like that. I mean, where am I going to go? There's no air out there, remember? Come on, Danny. Be reasonable here."

Even with all the energy-rich drugs now coursing through his body, Danny still wanted to lie back down, close his eyes, and drift off to sleep. Right now, he even considered pretending to go to sleep just to get rid of his other self.

"I am not going to vanish this time, Trooper Cole. Not now. Soon you will remember each and every vision. Not just yet though, I still think it's too early. You're getting close, so take comfort in that."

"Fine, I'm almost ready. Great. Now why don't you piss off and go bother somebody else."

Mr. Smith shook his head. "No, not yet. Not until I have told you this." His other self licked his lips. "You are, of course, aware that the Gizanti and that duplicitous Chaplain are only puppets. Their masters hope to achieve their hidden agenda that will affect every intelligent life-form within the galactic expanse."

"Leave me alone."

"The Empire have no idea what you or the other two signify. If that happens, then you might as well end your life right now for because you can guarantee that even with this alien invasion, the God-Emperor will stop at nothing to kill you." His other self stood up and walked over to the sleep-pod containing one of the soldiers. "Right now, the God-Emperor sees you as a curiosity, perhaps even a potential ally. This might change depending on how his next vision transpires." He stared at Danny. "As for the Gizanti… Who knows what their species want with you."

"What are you talking about? There's hardly any of them left. You heard what Cladinus said. The invading aliens have possessed their bodies. They're all as good as dead now. Cladinus doesn't want anything but to help us. He's grieving for his race; he has nobody left."

"You don't really believe that!" he spat. "You poor naïve fool. You really think that he took the ship to their home planet? It was just some colony world. He and the rest of his dead Gizanti pals are just leaves on a vast tree. Leaves fall off. Just watch yourself, Danny, because what you've been through so far is nothing compared to what's on the horizon. There is a huge amount going on behind the scenes. You remember that."

Danny jumped when the Gizanti walked through the door.

"You worry the Battle Sister when you have conversations with yourself," said Cladinus. He methodically checked the other sleep-pods before facing Danny. "This mission does not concern your fellow human comrades. Only myself and you will be leaving the Battle Sister. Please follow me." Without waiting for a reply, the Gizanti left.

He took one last look at the sleep-pods before racing after the huge alien. His racing mind went over every word that tumbled out of Mr. Smith's mouth while he followed Cladinus through the organic corridors of the quiet ship. The more he thought about the conversation, the more confused he became. Why couldn't he go back to how it was before the fucking visions? Danny was happy back then. Life didn't confuse him. He had his rifle, his squad mates, and his orders.

The alien entered the control room and stopped beside a jumble of ribbed pipes. It wasn't until he followed him into the room when he realised that all those pipes were connected to the Chaplain.

"What is this? What the hell have you done to him?"

"Do not by alarmed, Danny Cole. He is unharmed."

He approached the man, lying on the deck. It looked like two large pipes had literally swallowed his feet and ankles. Another smaller pipe covered his mouth and nose and another one entered his left ear. "Are you sure that he's okay?"

Cladinus nodded. "Yes, he is sleeping, much like you were doing a few moments ago. Only he is not talking to himself." The Gizanti's large orange arms waved in front of the corridor. "Watch."

A monitor beside Cole hummed to life, and he saw the Chaplain and a group of human fighters running down an ornate corridor full of paintings while avoiding blaster fire from unknown pursuers. It took him a moment for him to recognise the surroundings. "That's the Imperial Palace! Is this another vision? I mean, is what is happening on there going to happen?"

"The visions are sacred, Danny. Only a select few are worthy of experiencing such a revered event. What you see here is a simulation. We have inserted your Chaplain into a simulated scenario to extrapolate the most likely outcome."

The view altered, and Trooper Cole saw exactly what was chasing the Chaplain.

He gasped at the sight of three altered Gizanti racing along the corridor. "But, but I thought they were all dead." Danny stared at Cladinus. "How can this be?"

"My fellow Gizanti have been taken over by the alien invaders," he answered mechanically.

"Oh no, I'm so sorry about that." Danny felt something inside his head give, and he received the uncomfortable feeling that he already knew about this. Trooper Cole took a deep breath and willed the feeling away after remembering Mr. Smith's words about him getting close. "So this isn't a vision. Okay, does this not mean that the aliens will attack the Imperial world?"

The Gizanti sighed softly before turning around. "You need to follow me," he said. "We still have much to do."

Reluctantly, Danny turned from the monitor and followed the alien. His mind was full of questions, but he stayed silent. He believed that the answer to even one of his questions had the possibility to confuse him even more that he was already.

Cladinus led him into the hanger, and for the first time, Cole saw a large screen which displayed the environment outside the spacecraft. It didn't surprise him to see that nothing out there was remotely recognisable. "Where are we, Cladinus?"

"This is an ancient Gizanti colony world, my friend. Thankfully untouched by the alien invaders. It is also outside the Empire's sphere of influence." The alien pointed to a single combat suit already laid out. "I will leave so you can prepare. I shall return soon with sustenance."

As he started to climb into the combat suit, it didn't surprise him to notice his voice of reason leaning against the hanger bay door scowling at him.

"You are aware that your Gizanti pal is lying about the Chaplain. This ship could perform a million simulated scenarios without the human in the same amount of time that it takes you to put on that boot. Almost everything he says to you is either a lie or a distortion of the truth. You need to remember that."

He turned to Mr. Smith. "I've seen those altered Gizanti in a vision or dream."

"Didn't think it would take long for some of the walls to show signs of crumbling. Yeah, you saw them alright, and so has the Chaplain."

Mr. Smith glanced behind him. "Listen to me. Most alien races would cherish seeing the human race being crushed beneath the boot of an advanced alien race. You need to ask yourself why the Gizanti seem to be so eager to help."

Cladinus walked back into the hanger and gave Cole some dry, brown food cubes. "The Battle Sister has created these just for you. I think you will find them adequate for your needs."

He nodded before dropping them into his pocket. "You still haven't given me a good explanation as to why we're here or why none of the others are awake."

"I simply do not trust the other humans," he replied. "You are my friend. There is nothing else to say on the matter."

"Fine, so can you at least tell me why we're here?"

"All will be revealed, my friend." He waved his arms across a grey panel. "Prepare yourself, human. There are many dangers in this world."

The hangers doors receded into the ship's bulkhead and muted sunlight poured inside. Cole blinked before filling his lungs with the alien world's air. It felt good, really good. His system detected none of the usual pollutants generally found on an inhabited world. He walked out of the ship and placed his boots down of the pale-yellow, sandy surface. It almost felt like they'd just landed on a virgin world. Cole quickly scanned the horizon. He saw no sign of any civilisation. No buildings, no vehicles, and definitely no people. This wasn't a dead world; far from it.

The surrounding landscape was mainly yellow rock with scattered islands of plants, their thin blue stalks reaching up into the azure sky. Some of them had to be ten times his height; truly amazing-looking organisms. Broad, red leaves with glossy black globes hung from the tips of those tall plants. He watched them for a moment and saw that he had got it completely wrong. They weren't plants but the tendrils of some kind of carnivorous creature. He guessed that the bulk of the animal must lay under the earth.

He realised his mistake when he noticed colonies of bird-like animals circling the tall stems. If any of the flying creatures got too close, those stems whipped forward and curled over the unfortunate creature before it pulled its prize towards the ground.

The aerial creatures were the same colour as the Gizanti. Even from this distance, he could work out that they were at least three times larger than the creature stood next to him. He hoped they were carnivorous as well.

He saw a single sun, and on the other side, two moons, one significantly larger than the other one. Cole still found it hard to believe that the God-Emperor had no clue that this planet existed. They must still be in the Galactic expanse. They hadn't travelled far enough to have even reached the outer areas. What a beautiful and strange world. It could house millions of citizens with having plenty of land left over to help feed them as well as the rest of the Empire.

"Come. What we seek is not on the surface." The alien took off, moving at speed across the surface.

"Wait for me," he cried. Cole turned to see the ship lifting off.

"Do not worry, Danny, She is just moving to a safe distance."

"Safe from what? Those birds?"

Cladinus didn't answer, he just carried on moving. The alien didn't stop until he reached the mouth of a cave. Cole caught up with him. His question as to why the ship had left them stayed unsaid when he realised that this world wasn't quite as virgin as he initially believed. He knew from past experience that this cave was no natural formation. He lightly brushed his fingers down the smooth exterior. There was no doubt about it. Sometime in the past, this cave had been opened up using a plasma weapon. It had fused the rock, turning it into a material smoother than glass.

The alien reached into one of many folds distributed around his armour-plating and pulled out an Imperial blaster.

He gently turned the weapon around, wondering if there was any point in asking how the alien was able to acquire an SS80. Only the Empire's elite combat troops were issued with these. Cole pushed it into the empty holster and tried to stop himself from touching it.

"Try to stay quiet, human. The creatures that inhabit this system of caverns are sensitive to sound."

The blackness enveloped them. He kept his hand on the butt of his new weapon and the other on the smooth wall. He couldn't see or hear anything. For a creature three times Danny's size, Cladinus could move with remarkable grace. After a few moments, his eyes started to adjust to the change, and he began to make out rough shapes in the darkness.

They looked a little like strange rock formations. He counted over a dozen of them until the alien's bulk obscured what little vision he had, rendering him almost blind again. Cole spun around and faced the mouth of the cave and used what little light there was to search through his pockets, looking for a flashlight. He was losing it. Why didn't he do this before entering this stupid cave? To lose even one of his senses in a potentially hazardous mission was just asking for trouble.

The contents of the jacket yielded a host of devices some familiar, others not so. Until now, it hadn't occurred to Cole that the alien would have difficulty in distinguishing the difference between a compass and a Terran fusion heater.

He sighed to himself. Why should it be any different? After all, to him, every device in the alien ship looked like the inside of some dead animal.

Cole placed the items back in their respective pockets then brought out the few items that he didn't recognise, namely the ones which fitted into the "inside of a dead animal" category. It did occur to him that all he had to do was to ask Cladinus which one was a flashlight, but the alien told him to quiet. Also, Cole had no intention of asking anyone for help. After a few attempts, he managed to find one of these repulsive objects to do something other than cover his fingers in a thin film of sticky goo.

He almost dropped it when a pencil-thin green light shot out from one of the devices. He squeezed the cylinder's soft flesh-like surface and twisted it. The beam opened out, illuminating the inside of the cavern, casting everything in a dull green light. Cole turned back around and shone the beam over the walls, intending to examine those rock formations in greater detail.

Those seven rock formations were crawling all over the Gizanti! He pulled out the blaster and fired at the only creature not attacking Cladinus, hoping that the noise would scare the others away. The pulse of superheated plasma melted the creature's left arm. It screamed in agony, fell to the floor, and rolled around in the dust. Cole ran to Cladinus and booted the closest animal, not daring to fire again for fear of hitting the Gizanti.

The creature turned and snarled at him. Cole responded by reaching down, grabbing its ear, and dragging it off. Its long, hairy arms swept around, and Cole had to jerk his head back to avoid the long claws on its paws from leaving five deep lacerations across his face.

Cole pressed the muzzle of his SS80 against its stomach and fired once. Despite the gaping hole in its body, the creature still tried to slice open Cole's face.

"Push it against the wall."

Cole grabbed its throat and slammed the thing into the cavern wall, hoping the shock of the impact would at least stop it from trying to mutilate him. He didn't have to worry. As soon as its body touched the wall, fine strands of root-like material whipped out from the rock and pushed up through the melted hole in its body and spread out across its body. Cole jumped back when a couple of strands reached for his hand.

The stuff quickly covered its torso, arms, and legs. Cole had never seen anything like it before. He almost pitied the creature. He turned away when the fine strands expanded into its open mouth, grew up into its nostrils, and pushed hard points between its eyeballs and sockets.

"Thank you, Danny," said the alien.

He was back on his feet. There was no sign of the other creatures. Cole guessed that they must have run off into the darkness.

"They caught me by surprise. They had become more aggressive since I last visited here. It appears they had grown too. I do not remember them being so large." Cladinus brushed himself down. "Thank you for your assistance, Danny. I'm at your service." It was no longer moving; he guessed it must have died from loss of blood. It did not look alien at all. If anything, the dead creature reminded him of the great apes which once lived on old Earth, except, none of the holo images showed them with curved claws. He shivered at the thought of how close he'd been to dying. Come to think of it, if Cladinus wasn't covered in those thick-armoured plates, it could have been him lying on this cavern floor.

He got to his feet. If that had happened, what would have become of him? The alien's ship had taken off, presumably now in orbit around the planet. Would it have returned for him and the Gizanti body?

Cladinus picked up the ape-creature corpse and pressed it against the wall. Like before, strands of fibre started to grow over the dead creature.

"Feed and grow," he murmured. Cladinus turned to Cole. "I am sorry. I should have given you some warning of the dangers beforehand. I suppose it is redundant to advise you not to touch the walls, Danny." The alien gave a close approximation of a grin. "The plant that grows on the cavern walls secretes a digestive acid; it will not do your flesh any good at all."

"Are you going to tell me why a bunch of apes from my home-world just attacked us?"

"Who knows, my friend. Perhaps they got here during the first human expansion? Your species did not really care about species contamination all those thousands of years ago." The alien gave that grin approximation again before setting off once more, moving deeper into the cave system. "Remember not to touch the walls."

So the alien didn't tell him about the walls or the killer apes. In a way, he could understand that. Cladinus was an alien, and having different ideas about what consisted of danger came with the baggage. It's Mr. Smith's actions that annoyed Cole. Why did his voice of reason not give him prior warning instead of filling his head with hidden agendas?

Cole stopped walking and tried to keep a bubble of hysterical laughter from leaving his mouth. Did he just accuse his imaginary voice of withholding information? He needed to focus on the real and not dwell on the imaginary. He lifted his blaster and ran his finger across the barrel. This was real. Cole looked in disgust at the alien flashlight which still leaked out the sticky fluid. That was real too.

"We are here," said a distant voice.

He jerked his head towards the direction of the alien's announcement. He was real as well and so was this situation. Cole chided himself once again for allowing his mind to wander before hurrying through the caverns.

Cole discovered that he did not need the green beam from the organic flashlight in this new chamber. Several rectangular blocks embedded in the cavern ceiling flooded the area with harsh, white light.

"Where are we?" he demanded. Cole dropped the flashlight and approached the alien, his eyes roaming around this cavern. Unlike the rest of the cave system, this cavern almost felt like home. There was no way that the artefacts pushed to the edge of the walls were alien. He stopped in front of a metal box the same height as him and ran his fingers along the surface. He had no idea to its purpose.

"It was called a filing cabinet," said Cladinus. "Your species used them to store sheets of thin white material called paper."

"I thought you said it was a Gizanti colony?"

"It is, but it didn't always belong to us." The alien walked up to him, put his huge paws on Cole's shoulders, and gently turned him around. "Come, it is time to finish this and return to the ship."

The Gizanti took Cole over to another piece of equipment. Cole didn't need Cladinus to provide a description. He recognised the sleep-pods immediately, although these things were nothing like the models he had seen before. They were ancient, possibly thousands of years old. There were three of them, all arranged around a central pillar made of what looked like a primitive metal.

Cole looked inside one of the pods and grimaced at the blackened interior. Plastic had fused with bone and metal. "Somebody had died in here," he murmured. He gazed into the other two pods. The local wildlife had made short work the interior, but he saw no evidence of human occupation. "What happened here?" Cole looked straight at the alien. "Cladinus, tell me what happened here."

The Gizanti pointed to the central pillar. "Can you pass me that cube, Danny?"

He'd noticed it earlier but just assumed that it was one of the lights which no longer worked. Cole placed his fingers around the cube and pulled it out away from the surface. "There, now can you tell me what all this is about?"

"This is about a task that should have ended three thousand years ago." He gazed at the cube before returning his attention to Cole. "It remained unfinished because we changed, Danny." The alien abruptly turned around and left the chamber.

"Wait!" he cried, running after him. Cole scooped up the flashlight. "What is that supposed to mean?"

# CHAPTER TEN

They had politely asked Walish Din to retire to a sleep-pod before the ship began to cut through the black-weave. He had absolutely no idea what that was. Thankfully, his voice of reason had not left him. She explained that it was how these vehicles traversed the vast distances between the star systems, that they were able to fold spacetime and... At that point, he found his own mind folding spacetime as her explanation was as confusing as the ship captain's original question.

It was only when she told the Diannin that if they put him into a sleep-pod, then his influence on the staff would cease and they were likely to throw him out of the airlock. She also told him that most sentient species who did not have the adaptive treatment generally went insane.

Walish Din had not panicked or cried when his voice of reason had relinquished the news. Perhaps he was getting used to being given options which generally ended with either him dying in some gruesome fashion or losing his mind, sometimes even losing a limb. Instead, he stayed where he was, silently ordering his legs to stop shaking before refusing the ship captain's offer of a sleep-pod.

The human captain stayed with him and explained that as captain, the company took charge of the debt he'd incurred when he'd first had the treatment. He also expressed concern over his future career, considering the mess he'd just escaped from. The captain's voice trailed off. Walish Din guessed that the human realised that he had only lost his position whereas he had just lost his world. The silence only lasted a few seconds. The talkative human then said that he'd never heard of any Diannin leaving their world before.

The other voice in his ear echoed the captain's statement, saying that he was the first of his species to travel into space, and as she had no available data on how their bodies would react to the stresses caused when the ship left normal space, it was impossible for her to say whether he would survive the change.

Walish Din just wished that they would both stop talking to him, at least for a few moments. If his mind was about to be turned into mush, he would prefer to spend his last moments grieving over the friends and spawn donors that he had lost since this nightmare landed on his head.

The captain actually did stop talking but only to leave his side to inform those still awake that they were about to leave normal space. His voice of reason wished him good luck before she too left his side. Walish Din took a deep breath when the slight vibrations coming from the ship suddenly stopped. He felt his stomach turning in on itself before his ears popped.

The monitors on the bridge, displaying the exterior all cut out simultaneously. He saw the captain grip the holdall and he emulated his actions. The captain told him that the jump would only take a few seconds as they were only travelling to a system a few parsecs from this one. He opened his mouth again and then – Nothing.

Walish Din saw huge walking machines of death thundering towards him. He screamed and the view changed to a huge chamber with three metal coffins in the shape of Elasomog leaves in the middle of the chamber. He watched himself looking into one of the coffins. Walish Din shrieked when the coffin's occupier looked back at him. The person inside that metal contraption was Walish Din.

His eyes snapped open just in time to see the monitors were now showing the exterior once again. He shook away the effects of whatever he'd just experienced and looked around the bridge. Had his dream scream pierced through into reality? If it had, the captain gave no indication. Apart from his knotted-up guts, he didn't feel too bad. Walish Din wanted his voice of reason to appear so he could boast. It turned out that his species did not need any treatment to survive through whatever he'd just been through.

He saw no sign of the girl on the bridge.

"Oh no, not them! Can my day get any worse?"

Walish Din had no idea why the captain was so troubled. He followed his gaze and saw that the exterior now showed three huge dark grey objects in the external monitors. They looked very similar in shape to those coffins he saw in his waking dream.

"They're Imperial warships. Don't you know anything?"

"THIS STAR SYSTEM IS UNDER QUARANTINE. YOUR ORDERS ARE TO JOIN THE EVACUATION CONVOY IMMEDIATELY."

"They'll vaporise the ship if I don't comply!" he cried, rushing towards the front of the bridge.

Walish Din silently shook his head, knowing that the captain could not be allowed to alter his course. The captain slowed down until he stopped dead, a couple of metres from the front of the bridge. The man's eyes danced in their sockets.

"Time to leave."

He spun around to find his voice of reason stood beside him. "What's going on?"

"Your influence stops the captain doing anything other than what you originally asked him to do." She grabbed his arm and pulled him towards the door. "Come on, we have to get you to a lifeboat!"

"But you said if I leave, he'll alter course."

His voice of reason pulled the Diannin out of the hatchway. "Doesn't matter now. This ship has already defied the will of those Imperial warships. Even while you delay, they're already charging their cannons!"

She raced along the narrow corridor until the girl reached another hatchway. "Come on, move it!"

Before he ran after the girl, he heard the captain imploring with the Imperial warships to stand down, to give him a chance to make the necessary calculations. Walish Din groaned in despair, knowing that it wouldn't be just him and that captain who were about to die but the other people that this ship had rescued from their home planet. Just as he caught up with the girl, she set off again, this time turning left, heading towards the cargo hold. He should have stayed on his planet. What the hell was he doing here? Apart from getting a bunch of innocent people killed?

"Okay, I need you to climb into here," she said, pointing to the interior of a dark red cupboard. "Come on, we don't have much time left."

"What is it?"

"It's a lifeboat, you idiot," she shouted. "Now get inside!" she spun around. "Oh no, they're about to fire!"

Walish Din threw himself into the small space.

"Press the green button," she said.

He didn't even bother asking how she managed to climb inside without him noticing. Walish Din obeyed her command. The door rolled into place. He heard the sound of a dull thud and the lifeboat detached from the ship.

"Brace yourself."

Walish Din had no time to react to the girl's warning before the lifeboat's thrusters fired. He shrieked in terror as the lifeboat sped away from the main ship. Moments later, his world exploded into white light. By the time his eyes had adjusted, he saw that the ship was gone, only revolving balls of glowing red debris hinted that there was once anything occupying that space.

"They're all dead," he murmured. "And it's all my fault."

"Stop that," she said. "Stop that right now. It isn't your fault." She grabbed his chin and pulled him away from the view port. "Listen to me, Walish Din. They should have died on your planet and they would have if you hadn't ordered that captain to leave as he did."

"You don't know that."

The girl then kissed him. "It is a tragedy that those poor people had to die but right now, all that matters is for you and the other two to survive. Believe me. You three are the most important people in the Galactic Expanse. Without your continued survival, the fate of every sentient being hangs in the balance."

"No, I can't believe that. I refuse to believe it. I'm just a simple shepherd. All I know is glikgliks. You make me sound like I'm some kind of God."

She shrugged. "That's not far from the truth, my friend." She turned his head towards the viewport. "Look outside, Walish Din. Just look at what they're doing to this world."

Walish Din saw hundreds of spacecraft in orbit, some he believed were once part of the Terran Empire while others were of a design he'd never seen before. Not that this was too much of a surprise considering he'd never left his world until now. Still, the Diannin could still recognise some sort of pattern to the different ship designs. Walish Din also knew that their original owners were no longer in charge.

Like the orange dragons on his world and those huge metal walkers he had seen in his waking dream, the pipes and wires infested every ship. What made this utterly different was those pipes were not confined to their hulls. The vile-looking things reached out through the depths of space and joined up to the other ships, creating a vast web-like network around the planet.

He watched, dumbfounded, as those pipes pulled in another spacecraft and tethered it to the growing network. This one he did know as it was one of the Terran warships which destroyed the evacuation ship.

"Even if those warships hadn't been on patrol, the ship you'd travelled on wouldn't have made it to the surface."

The flexible pipes and wires ate through the warship's hull in dozens of locations. Hundreds of bodies flew out of the hull breaches. Walish Din wanted to be sick when he saw other, smaller, pipes reaching out and fastening themselves onto the ejected corpses.

"The aliens do not waste anything," she said.

He spun around. "Wait, what about us? I mean, what's to stop any of that stuff from latching onto the outside of this lifeboat?"

"That will not happen. They will sense your presence inside and avoid you. Trust me, I know this." She turned his head around again then sat beside him. "This is the first world they settled on, so their operation is more advanced than any other world. What you see here will happen to your world too, Walish Din."

"Why are they doing this? We haven't done anything to harm them!"

"I suggest you strap yourself in now. We're about to hit the atmosphere."

The lifeboat slipped between three interconnected ships. The pipes even brushed the outer casing of the lifeboat. He shuddered when he saw thousands of needle-thin tendrils whip out from the pipe and attempt to fasten on the lifeboat's hull, but just as she promised, as soon as they touched the skin, the stuff recoiled like it had been struck by lightning.

The ground rushed towards them like a bullet. Walish Din fought to hold in the scream, just hoping that he wouldn't be splattered across the side of this planet.

The girl wrapped her arms around his and pushed her warm body against his. "Calm yourself, they do slow down, trust me. I haven't let you down yet."

He decided to stay silent and close his eyes. Telling her exactly what he thought of her trust right now was probably a bad idea.

Walish Din felt the straps tighten just as his stomach launched up into his throat. He snapped open his eyes to see the scorched grey surface fill his viewscreen. "Wait, is the air okay? I mean, will I be able to breathe it?" It would be just his luck his he made it all the way to the planet's surface, only to choke to death in the toxic atmosphere.

"It's fine, stop worrying. Everything is going to be okay."

The lifeboat hit the ground with a slight bump. The straps fell away and the canopy slid back into the hull. Walish Din gingerly took one experimental breath. It didn't immediately kill him, so he decided that perhaps she was right after all. He turned to ask her what was he supposed to do now, but she'd done her usual disappearing trick again.

He climbed out of the lifeboat, unsure of what to do now. It felt weird to be safe, to know that nobody or nothing weird was trying to make him dead. Walish Din walked a few metres away from the lifeboat. He stopped then turned in a small circle, looking for anything that might resemble a village or town.

The landscape offered nothing but featureless desert. The only thing which broke the horizon was him and the lifeboat. He walked back to it, trying not to allow the built-up anger from spilling out. Oh sure, he was safe from any nameless pursuers, but unless he found food and drink, this stupid metal pod was likely to end up as his coffin.

This didn't make any sense. Why did she have to bring the lifeboat down to this remote location anyway? At least he assumed that it was under her control. Come to think of it, why did she have to go leave him just when he needed her most? He gripped the side of the lifeboat's cockpit. This just wasn't fair!

"Self-pity? Have you reduced yourself to this already?" Walish Din arched his back. It felt weird to hear his own voice without expecting a reply. A bit like old times, when he used to have such in-depth conversations with his flock. He smiled. Perhaps that wasn't the correct term as he spent most of his time complaining to the glikgliks over the tribe's apparent indifference to Walish Din's plight. He used to say that life wasn't fair to those stupid animals almost every day.

He looked around the landscape one more time in the hope that perhaps he had missed something during his initial scan. Walish Din stopped dead and gawked in disbelief at the sight of his voice of reason running towards him, with at least twenty orange dragons chasing her. It took him precisely three seconds for his shocked brain to inform him that this human was no figment of his imagination. She was the real thing.

"Why are you here?" she screamed.

Two of the huge monsters raised their staffs. "Get down!" Walish Din saw that she wasn't taking any notice, so he ran to the girl and threw his body against hers. They fell into the soft sand, just as the air a metre above his head burst into flames.

Walish Din turned his head and moaned in horror. His lifeboat was literally melting.

"You bloody idiot," she hissed. "Why are you even here? You're going to get us both killed!"

He looked up at the advancing dragons and watched them all point their staffs at him and the human.

# CHAPTER ELEVEN

What the hell were those things using? The Chaplain peered around the stone wall and silently prayed for the poor bastards who were once part of his diminishing unit of surviving Imperial Palace guards. Their hellish weapon had fused those three soldiers into the now melted plasti-steel wall.

He ducked down when the first altered Gizanti came into view. The fact that he was hiding behind the same plasti-steel constructed wall didn't escape his attention. It just wasn't possible. The palace walls were made from material designed to withstand everything from nuclear attacks to kinetic fusion bombs.

The Chaplain turned to face what remained of his team and showed the terrified sergeant at arms three fingers quickly followed by a fist. The man got the message and tapped the soldier crouched next to him on the shoulder. The soldier pushed the stock of his pulse rifle into his shoulder, aimed it at the wall in front of the Chaplain, and fired the three shot left the weapon. The Chaplain stood up and fired his SS80 directly at the first Gizanti before fleeing down past the five remaining soldiers.

His shot wouldn't have even scolded the alien never mind hurt it, but he just hoped that it would be distracted enough to allow him and his squad to reach the next turn without their awesome weapons turning any more of them into lumps of melted flesh.

He ran towards the next corner, painfully aware that they were all fighting a losing battle. Nothing they possessed were even slowing them down, never mind stopping the monsters. The Chaplain dived into the safe space. He rolled and pressed is body against the wall, firing continuously until the last of his men were behind him.

"There's several barrels of Lydrex propellant in the armoury," said the sergeant at arms. "We could blockade the next passageway, and as soon as they get close, we fire on the barrels." He nodded to himself. "There's no way they'd withstand that."

"Neither would we," said the Chaplain. He looked straight at the man's determined face. "Forget it. That stuff would filter through the entire palace, killing everything in here, including the God-Emperor. Is that what you want?"

The man shook his head. "Impossible. The God-Emperor is immortal, nothing can kill him. Not even these demons. Our lives mean nothing, our only task is to serve him."

"And we'll do that by wiping out every living thing in the palace?" The Chaplain got to his feet. "I applaud you for your ingenuity, but we need a better strategy."

"There is no other strategy, priest!" hissed the man. "We've thrown everything at them and nothing has worked." He looked behind him. Beyond the next door lies the God-Emperor's inner sanctum. I will not allow them to enter such a hallowed space.

"If they'll even go in that direction," murmured one of the house guards.

They had picked him up during the first frantic battle with the altered Gizanti. The very fact that Trooper Delaney was still alive and in one piece both physically and mentally surprised the Chaplain. The house guards were notoriously poorly trained.

"They might not come that way," he continued.

The plain truth of the matter was the Chaplain knew they'd be heading in this direction. Those ancient designers of this magnificent structure had built a vast maze within the several buildings which made up the palace. A maze impossible to decipher unless the individual had the microkey surgically implanted in their head. The walls moved randomly every dawn.

None of these preparations had stopped the invaders from getting closer and closer to their revered leader. They instinctively knew which direction to take. The Chaplain really wished there was some truth in the palace guard's blind optimism, but the increasing sound of the monsters' heavy footsteps told him otherwise.

"The doors to the inner sanctum, Sergeant. What do you think they're made out of?"

The man beside him shrugged. "The same stuff as the walls, I guess."

"Yeah, that's my guess as well." He stood up. "Sergeant, get your men through those doors. Once you're inside, bolt the door."

"What about you?"

The Chaplain patted the side of his blaster. "Like you said, Sergeant, our only task is to serve the God-Emperor. I will do that that by staying here and holding them off for as long as I am able. Now go."

He made sure that the soldiers had reached the double doors and entered the inner sanctum before turning back around to await the monsters. His sacrifice might buy them enough time to ensure that the God-Emperor is lifted to safety.

This was the right thing to do, despite his recent lapse in faith. The God-Emperor just had to live on, no matter the cost. Everything here could be rebuilt. As soon as that particular thought entered his mind, the Chaplain cried out in pain. He shut his eyes and slammed both hands to the side of his head to try to stop the agony.

The interior of the palace vanished. He saw another Gizanti and a human fighting some kind of furry animal before that two dropped away to be replaced with the image of the interior of some chamber dominated by three sleep-pods. The sergeant at arms and the other men were stood around them, all firing wildly at some unknown invader. Then, as quickly as the pain arrived, it left him.

He opened his eyes, picked up the dropped blaster, and pushed his shaking body against the wall. He had no idea what had just happened to him, nor did he want to know. The Chaplain got to his feet and took up position. Had he just had a vision or was something else at work?

"Focus on the task, Philip," he murmured.

He had to aim for the head, perhaps if he fired enough time in a single spot, perhaps one of his blasts might get through. The Chaplain heard the soldiers locking the door and pushing stuff against it. He might not last long, but the door should hold those monsters. He then frowned. The soldiers pushing objects against those doors were the only thing that he could hear.

"Where were they?" He stood up and ran out from his hiding place to find the corridor totally empty. The Chaplain slowly made his way back, his mind reeling at this new quandary. Had that guard been right about the monsters finding a different route? Had seemed too good to be true. If the altered Gizanti had gone in another direction, then the delay might actually give them the extra time needed to find some method of destroying the invaders.

He heard their distinctive staff blasts coming from somewhere inside the palace, telling him at they certainly hadn't retreated. Even so, where had they gone? He continued to carefully move back the way they came, looking for any new evidence of their passing. Their staff blasts echoed down the corridor. The Chaplain stopped dead. That sounded like they came from behind him, but how could that be?

He took a few more steps along the battle-damaged hallway of heroes then slowed down when his eyes focussed on an area of wall more damaged than the surrounding area. "No, this cannot be!" The Chaplain approached the melted mess with his guts folding over. He now knew why he couldn't see them; the monsters hadn't retreated, the bastards had simply cut through the wall!

Three more staff blasts echoed down the hole. He raced through the hole they'd made. He knew without conscious thought that the altered Gizanti had already found their own route into the inner sanctum.

It took him just seconds to reach their exit hole. He climbed through the melted plasti-steel wall and found himself standing inside the God-Emperor's revered Inner Sanctum. Even with these dire circumstances, the Chaplain still felt uncomfortable being in here without the express permission from the Revered Holy Order. Even approaching this area without permission generally meant instant death from the soldiers guarding this place.

He tried to shake away the guilt that came from the feeling of trespassing, like any of that mattered anymore. There wasn't anybody in the huge room, nobody alive anyway. The remains of two soldiers lay in front of the barricaded doors. Just like the others, the horrific damage from those staff weapons had fused them into the walls. The Chaplain turned away and said a silent prayer before tentatively moving away from the melted hole.

The remaining soldiers and the pursuing aliens must be somewhere else inside this place, yet he heard no more sounds of battling. The Chaplain wasn't sure whether this was a good thing. He sighed before examining this holiest of holy places. Due to his status, his knowledge of the palace stopped outside those doors. He had never been in here before, nor did he know the layout of this area of the palace or how large it was.

He wanted to leave this room and look for the others, but the images on the walls stopped him from going anywhere. The Chaplain approached the largest painting in the room. It was twice his height and depicted some battle between Terran shock troops and an alien force that he didn't recognise. Judging from the archaic uniforms and the primitive projectile weapons the Terran soldiers carried, this scene must have happened thousands of years ago.

Who were they? The aliens were half the size of the Terran soldiers, bipedal, with a long prehensile tail and covered in something with looked like a cross between fur and feathers. They certainly didn't look in any way aggressive. He remembered the tales told to him when he was a child about the horrors of the first expansion. His teachers told the class that once the great founders had perfected the ability to travel to the nearest star systems, the intelligent aliens they first encountered during this first expansion were all monsters. Each one more terrible than the next. They described creatures which made the Gizanti look like the cute, mammal-like creatures displayed in this painting.

The brutality displayed in the painting was just appalling. For a start, none of the aliens carried any kind of recognisable weapon. The Chaplain moved onto the next painting. In this, the Terran uniforms were a different design, plus the troops now carried crude-looking energy weapons. This battle happened possibility hundreds of years later, but the scene still followed the same vile pattern. In the painting, Terran dropships filled the crimson sky, their bay doors already open. Their cargo, elite squads of shock troops, were already on the ground, running across the rough terrain and cutting down anything in their path.

The aliens in this painting were reptilian in appearance. Apart from their bulk, which was significantly more than the Terran soldiers, they displayed absolutely no aggressive characteristics. They were plant eaters, even the Chaplain could tell that and yet, this didn't seem to matter. The Terran soldiers were still turning these terrified beasts into huge piles of blackened meat.

He stepped away from the appalling horror shown in these two and the many more paintings hung around this room. He felt ashamed to belong to the same species. What made his shame even worse was he knew these images were actually celebrating the genocide of all these creatures. His God-Emperor, the so-called immortal, wise, and benevolent ruler of their empire was nothing more than a tinpot dictator.

The thoughts which were running through his mind right now went against everything that he had believed in. He kept his gaze fixed to the floor and carefully walked over to the one official open doorway. As he stepped through into a large empty room, the Chaplain's mind began to suggest that perhaps what he had just witnessed did not actually happen. Perhaps they were part of a propaganda piece, designed to test a subject's faith. If that was the case, then he had failed.

He walked across the polished wooden floor, still fighting with his thoughts over the images that he had seen. If they were true, then it could help to explain what was going on right now in the Empire; that another unknown alien civilisation had been watching the Terran's despicable treatment of its fellow sentient creatures and decided to teach them a lesson they would never forget, to turn the tables on the so-called Terran Empire.

There was no way of knowing whether any of what he'd just seen was true. The only thing he should be concentrating on was his job, to ensure the safety of the God-Emperor. Nothing else mattered.

The sound of human voices drew him towards the only visible way out of the room. The Chaplain might not have been into these hallowed halls until now, but something deep inside now informed him that he had reached the end of his journey. He held the weapon in front of him and ran through the doorway.

He entered a surprisingly small chamber, the walls totally covered in hundreds of alien hides. The thick, stench of decay coming from the hides made the Chaplain want to throw up. He took another step into the room and finally saw the true face of the beloved God-Emperor. Right in front of him were three sleep-pods, arranged around a central pillar. Only one of the sleep-pods was occupied. The Chaplain looked inside to find the wizened face of a man who should had died thousands of years ago staring back at him.

There were no signs of the other humans or the altered Gizanti.

Philip Diocolis, Prime Chaplin of the third Imperial Order, opened his eyes and looked straight at the dark red pulsating bulkhead directly above him. It took him a couple of moments for his senses to come back fully. He was in his sleeping quarters on the Gizanti ship. The Chaplain shook away what remained of that vision or dream and sat up. This didn't feel right. Why wasn't he in one of the sleep suppression beds? Wait, never mind that, his last waking memory was this living ship growing over his feet!

Was that a dream as well?

"You seem preoccupied, Chaplain. Is this a bed time? If you want, I could come back once you are fully rested."

He gripped the sides of the bed to stop himself from falling onto the floor. Oh not her, not now. The Chaplain sprung to attention and attempted to look sombre in the presence of the Empire's High Priestess. "Apologies. I was not expecting you."

"Yes, so I see." Her holo walked to the front of his bed. "There has been a change to your orders. You are to take this obscene space vehicle to the Augustus shipyards. Once arrived, you are instructed to destroy the facility."

He nodded. This confirmed that the God-Emperor and Cole had shared the vision of the altered mechs laying waste to the area around the palace. What about the vision he'd just shared, with those Gizanti laying waste to the palace itself?

"Once you have ensured that nothing in those shipyards is capable of threatening the Imperial home-world, you are to serve sentence on the minor heretic before returning home."

The High Priestess then gave him a smile that could have broken the hearts of the thousands of teenage boys who followed the woman on her personal vid channel. It almost made her shocking words sound perfectly acceptable.

"You have done well, Philip. Expect to be rewarded for your bravery and dedication to the Empire. Perhaps even a position within the Revered Holy Order? Relax, Philip, you have done better than we expected."

He bowed, not entirely sure what he had done to receive such a revered gift. "Glory be to the Empire and our revered Emperor," he said. "May his reign last for another..." The holo vanished before he could complete the traditional acknowledgement.

What was he supposed to do now? How could he possibly order the men to execute the so-called minor heretic? The picture of his God-Emperor lying in that sleep-pod ran through his mind. He had pledged his unswerving devotion to the God, meaning that he had no other choice to carry out his order, no matter how he felt.

The door to his private quarters slid open. Philip bit his bottom lip and rested his hand over the butt of his private blaster. If the visitor turned out to be Cole, then he would kill him where he stood and worry about his damned soul some other time.

"You looked a little troubled," remarked the Gizanti. "May I enter?"

"I'd rather you didn't. In fact, the very thought of company repels me."

The large alien took no notice of the Chaplain's reply and walked into the room anyway. He ground his teeth in annoyance; obviously, this creature believed it was his right to go anywhere on this obscene blasphemous container of alien filth without asking permission.

Cladinus approached the monitor in front of the Chaplain and waved his large hand in front of the screen. "I have something to show you, Chaplain. Something which might persuade you from acting out an instruction that could have serious repercussions."

The picture of a light blue sky filled the monitor screen. The image panned across the horizon. Philip leaned forward, growing more and more excited at the sight of the single large moon sitting above a distant mountain range. He saw another smaller moon before the camera stopped in front of a group of impossibly tall, thin plants. "I don't understand why you are showing me the images of some planet, Gizanti."

"Do you not recognise it?"

He shook his head. "No, should I?"

"Granted, when your species owned it, there was only the one large moon. Once we claimed possession, my ancestors removed a smaller moon from one of the other planets in the star system and placed it into orbit to help simulate our true home."

"Are you telling me that this is old Earth?" He leaned forward and silently groaned when he saw the minor heretic come into view. This had to be very recent, which made his next question of how old these images were. He watched him and the camera wearer, who he assumed to be the large alien, travel across the unfamiliar landscape. The study of old Earth, its geography, flora and fauna, the ancient civilisations, and the history were all an intrinsic part of the church teachings. Given time, the Chaplain hoped to discover whether this was one of the alien's deceptions, and if that proved to be the case, then it would be his sworn duty to punish the Gizanti for high blasphemy.

It would be difficult to work out if the Gizanti was telling the truth. Those mountain ranges could be anywhere on the planet's continents. Guessing from the flora and fauna work not work either as it was clear that the aliens had introduced species not indigenous to Earth. He resorted to the only method remaining. The Chaplain asked, "Whereabouts is this?"

"I believe that this part of the planet was once called the United States of America."

He nodded, still not really believing the alien. "Are there any humans left on the planet?"

"No, the little remaining number fled before the deadline ended."

"What deadline? Our forefathers left the old planet during the first of the great expansion. Everybody knows that."

"Is that what they told you? I supposed these were the same teachers who reassured you that during this first expansion, every alien species you annihilated were twelve-foot, armour-plated monsters who fed about the flesh of your young children?"

Embarrassed, the Chaplain turned back towards the monitor and focussed on their progress through the caverns. The green light picked out a number of irregularities which made him suspect that they were not in any natural formation. For a start, he was sure there was some form of faded writing, half-visible under all that creeper-like vegetation. Also, a number of times, the 'rock' looked a little too straight, suggesting that perhaps they could be travelling through a man-made construction.

His suspicions were confirmed when Cole and the alien reached the final chamber. The bright lighting showed the full room in all its glory. Animal pelts covered the wall. The Chaplain turned away from the sight only to find himself staring at another set of three sleep-pods, arranged around a central pillar. He watched, with his mind reeling what this could mean while Cole took a small cube out of the central pillar. He looked straight at the alien. "What does this mean?"

"The machine is called a Trinity Cradle, Philip. It has the power to expand the consciousness of the occupants. It can give them God-like abilities. Can you possibly conceive of how this one device altered your planet's future? You went from some minor sentient species with hardly any knowledge of what lay beyond your own star system to becoming an utter scourge amongst the Galactic Expanse with only a couple of millennia. Philip, the device was never designed for one occupant. What was supposed to bring in an era of peace and enlightenment across the Galactic Expanse, instead, gave us terror and genocide."

"So the one I saw in my vision was a copy?"

The alien nodded. "Yes."

"What about the pictures of the Terran forces massacring all those aliens? Did that really happen as well?"

"I'm afraid, that your race is guilty of more counts of genocide than any other species in the past half a million years."

"I see," he replied, although he didn't. The Chaplain looked closely at the ancient sleep-pod while remembering the one in his vision. He then looked at the Gizanti. "So, this is retribution? Another, more advanced alien species discovered what the Empire had been doing for the last three thousand years and decided to do something about. Okay, that makes sense. What I don't understand is why they targeted your species as well."

The Chaplain had to catch his breath when he felt waves of misery rolling off the alien. "We tried to tell you. My ancestors attempted to put you back on the path to enlightenment, even to the point of threatening to take away your home-world. What we did not understand at the time was that most of your violent species either left for the stars or killed each other. The number of humans on your planet were depressingly low. We gave you an ultimatum, which was ignored, so our ancestors took away your planet, but even that didn't stop you. By this time, your God-Emperor was already installed in his new home. Then we changed, our own species underwent a transformation and adopted the notion of non-intervention."

"I can understand why they changed the story," he muttered. "We don't really have a good relationship with aliens with advanced technology."

"You don't have a good relationship with any alien race, my friend."

"So what do I do now?"

"That is your choice. Either obey your God-Emperor's orders, or follow your heart and do what you think is right."

# CHAPTER TWELVE

Her hair should have been a darker brown, and she certainly shouldn't be so small, but the girl was definitely the same human who had helped to transform his otherwise sedentary life into a complete nightmare. It was strange how easily he could tell them apart now. A few days ago, Walish Din couldn't even distinguish between genders.

Maybe it wasn't that strange after all considering the amount of time he'd been spending with the aliens. The strange part of this situation just had to go to his current frame of mind. Had his emotions taken such a battering that even the sight of so many orange dragons carrying their silver staffs didn't even cause him to wet himself in terror?

"Why bother running when there is nowhere to run to?" he heard himself mutter.

"Oh God, what the hell are you doing here?" screamed the girl. "You should have gone somewhere else. Now they'll be able to kill the pair of us."

The words 'I'm here to save you' now sounded utterly ridiculous, but it didn't stop his stupid mouth from repeating them.

She dived forward and wrapped her arms around his waist just as four dragons aimed their staff weapons at the pair of them. Walish Din was staring death right in the face and yet he still felt no fear.

"You're here to save me?" she announced. "Sure you are."

The four orange dragons fired simultaneously. The blasts which he believed would be his last sight hit an invisible wall in front of them. The huge wave of bone-melting heat dispersed around the two people.

"How did you do that?"

"I have no idea, but it's been keeping me alive. At least up to now. So you had better have something special, you furry alien, because I won't be able to do that again."

Walish Din didn't have a single idea what she was talking about. He just lay on the floor, watching those orange monsters approach while his numb brain insisted that he should be dead right now.

"Come on!" she screamed. The girl grabbed the front of his jacket and shook him. "Snap out of it. You must be able to do something to help!"

This one was a little more excitable than the girl who lived in his head. Although she was right. He got onto that spaceship and persuaded the captain to change his course. Could that work again? Walish Din got to his feet and helped the girl up before calmly walked towards the advancing line of orange dragons. Three of them had already aimed their staff weapons at him. As he raised his own arm, Walish Din felt every muscle in his body lock up. The sensation only lasted for a split second, but it was enough to make him stumble.

The three orange dragons stumbled too. One of them twisted around and fired his staff into the line of the armour-plated monsters right behind him. The blast obliterated five of the creatures, but it didn't stop them from advancing.

The other two had somehow regained their balance. Their staff weapons swung around to aim at him again.

"I'm not going to die like this!" he screamed. "Not on this planet. You are to killing me like you did to my tribe." Walish Din dug both his feet into the sand. He glared at the remaining monsters before raising both his arms into the air.

Every single orange dragon ground to a sudden halt. They lowered their staff weapons then lowered their heads before they shuffled backwards, creating a wide path through the middle of them.

He didn't even try to explain what was happening. The Diannin picked the human out of the sand, kept a tight hold of her hand, then ran as fast as he could through the aliens. Walish Din tried not to focus on the fact that the view of even more desolate wasteland filled his vision. He'd bought them about a minute more time to keep breathing. This featureless desert offered nothing to shelter behind.

Walish Din carried on pumping his legs, praying that something might happen that didn't involve a painful death. He risked a glance over his shoulder to discover that even if they had stayed by the lifeboat and take shelter behind that, the orange dragons would have still roasted their bones. He bit his bottom lip and silently wished for the other human, the imaginary one to make an appearance. She'd know what to do.

"Don't look so distressed, my furry friend," she said.

The girl turned his head away from the melted remains of his lifeboat and pressed her lips against the tip of his nose. "Thank you, and I'm sorry for calling you an idiot."

He wondered if this was her way of clearing the air between them before those staff weapons melted them too. Even as she moved her head away, he saw the surviving monsters were already getting ready to fire again.

"Come on, we best keep moving. I think I can deflect another blast now." She grabbed Walish Din and pulled him to the left.

He dare not look behind him now; he just hoped that she was right. Also, he now wanted his last image to be of the human and not his execution squad. Walish Din felt something warm brush across his back, and he knew that the human had just saved their lives one more time.

She stopped running grabbed both his hand then pulled him to the ground. "Okay, when I say so, you need to roll towards me. Do you understand?"

"Yes."

The orange dragons were now some distance away, but they were now catching up. Did she expect them to start burrowing into the sand? He wanted to tell her that his species were not subterranean dwellers. Come to think of it, he had no idea that humans possessed any burrowing ability. He wanted to tell her this, but before he got the first word out, the human told him to roll and then, just for good measure, grabbed his shoulder and savagely pulled him towards her.

The ground vanished from under his body. He instinctively pushed out his arms to slow his descent, but by the time the tips of his fingers brushed against the hard-packed sand, Walish Din had already reached the bottom before he had a chance to cry out.

The girl jumped in after him. She placed her hand over his mouth. "You need to stay quiet; the Gizanti can track through noise."

It was all very well for her. Humans probably saw in the dark like the spine-raptors from his planet. He heard her rummaging through her clothing before he found some of the darkness had vanished thanks to the dim yellow light coming from the end of a flashlight. That made Walish Din feel a little better about this whole situation. Having some alien girl being able to see in the dark on top of everything else would just finish him.

The young Diannin followed the human and her weak flashlight through the dry, hot tunnels, trying to keep his feet from tripping himself up. Somewhere in the distance, the sound of those horrific staff weapons cut through the silence. Every time one of them fired, Walish Din jumped. He couldn't help himself. He guessed that now it looked like he was finally safe, the shock of everything that he'd been through decided to pay him a visit.

"Are you okay?"

The Diannin hadn't realised that the girl had stopped moving. He stopped dead then leaned back against the wall to catch his breath. He followed the girl's beam as she played it over the hard-packed sand. "Are we okay to talk now?"

"As long as we don't start shouting and jumping up and down, we should be okay now. Those freaky Gizanti are pretty stupid."

"Is that what they're called?"

She smiled. "Don't you know?"

Walish Din kept his mouth shut, deciding not to tell her that he'd been calling them orange dragons since he first saw the monsters. He did find himself starting to shake though, and no matter what he tried, the shuddering refused to leave him.

"Oh, you poor thing!" She put her hands on his shoulders and gently pushed him to the ground before wrapping her arms around his body. "Shit, I'm sorry, it's just struck me that you're a herd species." She pulled back and gazed steadily at him. "What's your name?"

"Walish Din," he managed to say.

"I'm guessing that your home-world is experiencing the same disaster as what's happening here?"

"They're birthing worlds."

"Who told you that?" she snapped.

Walish Din found enough energy to smile at her. "You did."

"How can that be? We have only just met." She shook her head. "No, don't worry about it; since when has anything these past few days made sense anyway? So you managed to escape from your planet while the freaky Gizanti were going around and melting everyone, convince some pilot to travel here, and then slip through that web they're constructing around the planet?"

"I just wish I knew why." Until now, Walish Din hadn't even asked his imaginary human girl why it was so important to link up with the real version. It certainly wasn't to save her life as she'd obviously been doing that quite well up to now. "Have you been seeing people who aren't there or dreaming of strange far-away places?"

She shook her head. "No. I've been too busy spending the last three days running for my life to notice invisible people and have spaced-out dreams." The girl gently removed her arms. "I think it's accurate to say that I've not had the best days since coming to this crap-hole of a planet."

"Oh, so you are from here?"

"You are joking? This place is literally on the edge of the Galactic Expanse. There's nothing here but sand, the odd trader like me, and the natives."

"The blue ones?"

She nodded. "For someone who has only just got here, you sure know a lot about where you are, Walish Din."

He cast his mind back to his vision. Walish Din placed his fingers around her slender hand. "You were inside an eating establishment when the big orange aliens entered the city. An old human standing next to you kept muttering that they couldn't be Gizanti." He swallowed hard. "That's the point when you first saw those monsters fire upon the two fleeing natives."

"Stop!" she gasped, pulling her hand away. "No more. I've had enough freaky and weird stuff happening to me for some total stranger to start telling me my past. Come on, we'd better keep moving." The girl stood up and started to move away.

"Wait. At least tell me how you managed to find me. I mean, it can't be a coincidence that you just happen to be right at the place where I landed."

"I don't know. I mean, I've been using these snake trenches to move from town to town while trying to find some way off this damn planet."

After seeing what had happened to that Imperial warship before his lifeboat slipped through that rapidly closing net, it's probably best that she hadn't been able to get a lift. How long would have lasted if she hadn't been here to save him? It's probably best that he didn't think about that too much either. "They're really called snake trenches?"

"It's not as silly as it sounds, Walish Din." She placed her fingers against the sand wall. "These tunnels really were carved out by huge snakes." The girl giggled when he pulled a face. "Oh, don't look so scared, they don't exist anymore. The native species hunted them to extinction decades ago." The girl reached into another one of her pockets. "It's the sole reason why I came to this otherwise miserable planet. You see, the Slitherline can't get enough of these little things." She opened the lid on a small box and showed him the contents.

He frowned at the sight of hundreds of tiny, pale worm-like organisms frantically trying to climb up the sides of the box. Walish Din moved his hand a little closer only for her to slap it away.

She closed the lid. "That's not a good idea. These are flesh-eaters. It doesn't bother the blue guys though; just the hint of a smell coming from these gross things sends these normally peaceable creatures into a blood-lust frenzy."

He wanted her never to stop talking. The sound of her melodious voice helped to smooth off the rough edges of his jittery feelings. "So, you're not from this world. Okay, so how did you find out about this place?"

"No, you're right there, I certainly am not from here. My world is close to the Imperial centre. This is the first time that I've travelled so far from the inner systems. I still don't believe that I'm here, running through these snake trenches on this dead-end backwards planet. I honestly thought that I'd be gone from here the day after I arrived."

"You do not have a high regard for this world?" He didn't rate the place either. Somehow, he thought that all the other planets would look so different to his world, that they'd be strange and exotic places, full of alien creatures that looked so different to anything else he'd seen.

"I don't want to insult you, Walish Din, as I know your species live on a frontier world, but no, I hate this planet, and not just because of what I've gone through either. I'm a trader, remember, and the less advanced races out here only seem to care about whether the next harvest is going to fail. How can a mind like that appreciate the complexities of planetary market trading?" She sighed. "Why am I even trying to explain this? I bet you're a farmer too."

"No, I'm a shepherd."

"Right, and how is that any different?"

Walish Din decided not to mention that the Imperial prospectors had never bothered to visit his backwards planet. He thanked all the spirits roaming the Plains of Gopin for this fortitude as every Diannin knew of the vast wealth of precious metals lying under their ground. They also knew of the terrible consequences of what happened on other mineral rich worlds when that knowledge reached the God-Emperor. He knew a lot about trading, certainly a lot more that this human gave his credit. He decided not to bother mentioning that too. "It still doesn't explain to me why you are on the planet. Unless this is where you chose to take your vacation?"

"Very funny," she muttered. "Come on, we'd better find somewhere better than this before it gets dark." She started to walk away from him. "You know, just in case the blue guys were lying about the snakes. In the morning, we can try to work out a way of getting off this damned rock before it's too late."

Walish Din hurried after her. For a start, the girl possessed the only light. The thought of being stuck down here in the dark made his blood turn to water. "Wait, please, you're going too fast. Please, tell me why you're here. I know you said you came to this planet to give the blue guys your worms, but you still haven't explained how you heard about them." When she stopped talking, that jittery feeling came back with vengeance.

"I was in this bar," she said. "Minding my own business, swirling the remains of the cheapest drink in the place around the bottom of the glass. I'd been in there for over two hours, trying to think of some way to find enough credits to stop the Imperial auditors from taking everything I owned away from me." The girl shined the flashlight under his eyes. "Thanks to a few unfortunate deals that I'd made in the past, as well as two months of having no job to do, I really was down to my last couple of credits. Anyway, so there I was, generally feeling sorry for myself when this guy sits next to me. He said hello then bought me a drink. Usually, I would have told anyone making a pass at me to clear off but, like I said, I had no more money to buy myself another drink."

"What was he called?"

"I remember that he had such pretty eyes."

His heart started to beat a little faster. This human was about to repeat the name she said in his first vision.

"I can't quite remember. I was too busy looking at his eyes."

"Was it Danny?"

Her own eyes lit up. "Yes, that's it. How did you know? Wait, don't answer that. I don't want this day to get any stranger. Well, we started talking and he told me about the Slitherline."

Walish Din tried not to laugh. "Let me guess, he just so happened to have a container of these worms and needed a plot and a ship?"

"He said he would split the profits in half. It sounded like a great offer, and at that moment, I had no other choice. It was either take this job or wait for the Imperial auditors to take all my stuff. Looking back, he must have bewitched me with his lovely eyes." The girl shrugged. "Not that it matters anyway. I'm not sure what matters. After what I've seen those things do on the planet, I very much doubt that there will be any Empire to return to, even if we do get off this rock."

Some great cosmic deity had spun a web which spanned the whole Galactic Expanse and they were both caught on the threads. He suspected that the other human, this Danny, could also be stuck inside this web too. He made his hand into a fist and smacked it against the sand wall.

"What the hell are you doing now?"

"Shaking the web," he answered. "Don't you see it yet? Nothing we have gone through had transpired by accident. You see, I don't really believe that this Danny was really there in that bar." He leaned forward until his face was just inches from her nose. "I also believe that he hasn't left you either."

"You've lost your mind," she retorted before pushing him back. "I don't even know why I'm talking to you. You're just some simple shepherd who's in the same amount of shit as me." The girl sank to the floor. "I just want to go home. Is that too much to ask for?"

This shepherd might not have come from an advanced species like this human, but that hadn't stopped him from achieving something which had initially sounded impossible. Her journey hadn't been as traumatic as his, but Walish Din suspected that her nightmare began once the aliens invaded. He sat down opposite the girl. "Every person I knew at home is now dead."

"I'm sorry. I should have been more careful with choosing my words."

"There's no reason to be sorry. If you hadn't been there to help me, I would have most probably died with them." Walish Din didn't expect the girl to answer him, so he wasn't shocked by her silence. "I bet he vanished at the same time as you saw the lifeboat plummeting to the ground."

She nodded.

The girl was nothing like the one who'd shouted, dragged, insulted, and threatened him into following her requests and orders. Looking back, if she hadn't been so forceful, Walish Din doubted that he would have made it this far. Did this mean that the imaginary Diannin living in her head would have acted in a similar manner? The deity had shaken his vast web and brought the pair of them together, presumably to wait for the third one, the other human, Danny. Surely, there must be more to it than that? If that was the only reason, then why did she have to come all the way out here? It would have been much easier and safer for him to travel to where she originated from.

Walish Din would have liked that.

He stood up, put his hands around her wrists, and pulled her onto her feet. "If this is another birthing world, then there must be somewhere on this planet where the aliens had deposited the incubators? I bet you know where they are as well."

"Please don't make me take you there," she whispered.

Her sudden emotional change took him completely by surprise. Where had the human's brashness gone? It then occurred to him that perhaps her imaginary Diannin treated the human in the same way as his imaginary human female. Walish Din would like to meet the deity who built this web and smash him in the face.

"Don't you start begging already. We're both here for a reason, and it's about time you faced up to this notion." He snatched the flashlight out of her hand. "Where did you land your ship? I assume that it's still intact?"

"That's going to do any good. You know we won't be able to get off the surface. Not now, not with that cage they're building around it. Why did I stay here? I must have been insane."

"You sure do ask a lot of impossible questions, human. I also notice that you're filled with quite a lot of regret." He let go of her and carried on walking while shining the flashlight over the tunnel surface. "Where did you land your ship?" he repeated.

"I almost died during the landing. Something went wrong this the guidance computers as soon as I hit the atmosphere. I still done know how I managed to land the ship safely. Oh, don't worry, I checked it couldn't find anything wrong with it. Not that I've been able to check the ship recently." She took a deep breath. "Those human incubators appeared all around my damn ship! This was obviously before I discovered these snake trenches."

"Again, he shakes his web."

"Pardon?"

"Nothing. I'm guessing that these trenches will take us to your ship?"

"Yeah, I guess so. Why?"

Should he tell the human the idea that came to him a few moments ago? "I believe that there's a greater power at work here, and I think that whoever is controlling our fate has brought us here to do something." He paused. "From what you have seen of the power from these invading aliens, do you think that the Empire will be able to defeat them?"

It took her a few moments before she answered him. The girl nervously licked her lips. "They have displaced thousands of humans from one planet to another. They have managed to turn a race of creatures millions of years older than the human species into soldier slaves." She looked up. "And now they're making an impenetrable shield around this world. They're probably doing the same to their other conquered worlds as well. No, I don't think the Empire stands any chance of defeating them."

Walish Din followed her example and licked his lips too. "You are obviously aware that there are countless alien races out there would welcome the Empire's extinction."

"So would many humans, Walish Din."

"Does that include you?"

"I've never been a huge fan of the Empire," she admitted. "Thing is, what's going to happen if or when these aliens do crush the Empire? What's going to happen then?"

He hadn't thought about that. The humans hadn't really bothered much about his species; they certainly hadn't sent a swarm of orange dragons to kill everyone he had ever known.

"Why are you still here, Walish Din? For crying out loud, stop it with the thinking and get on with your plan!"

He spun around at the sound of the new but familiar voice to find the other human female standing directly behind him, hands planted on her hips while glaring him.

"The only reason why the humans haven't bothered with your species is because you don't interest them in any way. They would if your little secret had reached the ears of anyone important. Believe me, they would have literally wiped you out before bringing in their machines to extract everything of value from your world."

"Who are you talking to, Walish Din? Is it her? Is it the one who looks like me?"

"Now stop it with the hesitating and get on with it!"

He watched her image grow translucent before finally disappearing. Walish Din turned around, pushed past the girl, and strode down the tunnel. "We're wasting time," he said. "Show me where your ship is."

She took the flashlight back. "Fine, we'll do that, but I just hope that your species knows how to run, because even if you do fall back, I won't be coming back for you." Having said her piece, the girl took off, leaving him alone in the dark.

He watched the glow from the flashlight grow dimmer and dimmer as she increased the distance between them.

"Are you not going to catch her up?" asked a voice.

"I thought you would appear once she had gone. I have some questions and I expect straight answers and not riddles."

"You're going to lose the girl if you don't run after her, Walish Din!"

"For a start, you can tell me exactly who you are, because you're not that girl, and you certainly aren't a figment of my imagination."

She laughed. "Some of me has been taken from you, my friend. Just like a portion of your new human friend was used to create her guardian. The rest? Well, who can say where that came from. Perhaps your web-creating deity has something to do with that. Before you hit me with another question followed, no doubt, by a barrage more, my purpose is to ensure your survival, to make sure you reach your final destination in one piece. Something which won't happen if you carry on delaying."

Before he had a chance to ask her any more questions, the girl disappeared, leaving him totally alone. Walish Din smiled to himself before setting off walking. He didn't run after her, knowing that somewhere along this tunnel, she would be waiting for him. He knew this, just as he knew that his imaginary girl would return the next time he faced imminent danger.

He walked for quite some time before he began to spot the faint change in the blackness. The glow from her flashlight grew brighter. Walish Din expected her to start shouting at him, but the girl kept her silence, simply moving the light from the floor to his face when he stopped beside her.

"This is the place."

He nodded, noting the tremor in her voice. The girl was scared of what was above their heads. Until now, he hadn't allowed his mind to dwell on the details of his plan. Perhaps that was a good thing. Walish Din was still, at heart, a creature which shied away from confrontation. Thinking ahead would have probably have locked up his mind by now.

"We have to stop whatever is in those incubators from breaking out," he said, watching her expression change from anxiety to utter terror. "That is why they have brought us to this world. It's the only thing which makes sense."

"You have lost your mind, Walish Din. What do you mean by they? Is this something to do with your web again? I hope that you're aware of the kind of animal that spins a web. So this means that we're just flies, waiting to be eaten."

"Have you quite finished?"

"I'm a trader, not a soldier, and it's pretty obvious that your species doesn't have a single warrior cell in your body."

He shrugged. "Appearances can be deceptive," he replied, pointing to the pocket where she stashed her box full of worms. "The blue aliens that I saw in my vision looked docile to me, and yet you say that all that changes when they smell those worms."

Before the girl opened her mouth to vomit out a load more reasons not to go, he kicked out a hole in the sand wall at the height of his knee before repeating the same action on the other side. He took a deep breath then started to climb. The top of his head pressed up against some kind of barrier. It wasn't sand, that much he knew.

"You have to push yourself out right at the edge of the wall," she said. "That's how the trenches work."

He complied with her reply and found himself staring at the feet of hundreds of humans, all as still as stone statues. He now understood the girl's reluctance to continue. He felt that her terror has just jumped into his body. It took him a couple of moments to find the courage to swing the rest of his body out of the trench.

Three rows of human statues stood in front of the girl's ship. The vehicle's hull glinted in the moonlight. Walish Din blinked, until he noticed that this planet's star had sunk below the horizon.

He watched the humans for a couple more seconds just to make sure that none of them were moving before he returned to the edge of the trench. He dropped down and ran his fingers along the sandy soil and stopped when he found what he was searching for. Walish Din gripped the edge of the trench covering and pulled it up to reveal the female human staring up at him.

"There's no Gizanti up there?"

"If there was, I wouldn't be up here. I'd be diving back in that trench." He reached down and helped her up. "Come on, let's get this finished."

"Get what finished? You still haven't told me what you plan to do."

Walish Din walked up to the closest human. Like all the others, he wore no clothing, none of them possessed any hair, and a thin film of shiny oil covered their bodies. He kept his fingers clear. He had the feeling that a break in the covering would bring every orange dragon on the planet here.

His inspection discovered something else amiss. The skin covering this human's stomach was not opaque like the rest of his body. He was sure that this was not normal. He leaned a little closer and saw several spherical egg-sized objects swimming around in a thick pale fluid. Walish Din glanced over his shoulder. The girl's eyes bulging in their sockets confirmed that this wasn't part of their species anatomy. "This must be what the orange dragons are guarding. I wonder what they do once they hatch?"

"I really don't like it here," she muttered.

He threaded his way through the humans, heading towards the girl's spaceship. "I hope your species can run," he said, smiling, "because even if you do fall back, I won't being returning for you." Walish Din reached the ship then turned around. "Don't let your body touch theirs," he said. "We're not ready for the orange dragons just yet." He waited for the girl to reach him then patted the hull. "I take it that the box you're carrying are samples and the main delivery is in here?"

"You know it is, Walish Din," she said miserably. "Look, this is not going to work. You know that. More than likely, we'll both end up as worm food."

"I need you to release your cargo."

She pushed past the Diannin and scrambled onto the hull of her ship then walked along the roof. The girl kneeled down and opened a grey panel. "You staying down there, Walish Din? As soon as those worms are released, you're going to be their first lump of fresh meat."

How stupid could he be? Walish Din followed her example and climbed onto the roof of her cargo ship. "Sorry."

She turned to him. "It's not too late to look for another solution. Once I activate the release clamps, there will be no backing away."

"Do it."

The girl fought back a sob. "Shit."

She inputted a series of numbers then slammed the panel shut. Sure enough, the bay doors slid back and an auto-arm lifted four cubes out from the inside of the ship and deposited them on the sand. Walish Din crawled forward, held the edges of the hull, and watched the lids open. As soon as the moonlight hit the worms, they frantically wiggled out and dropped onto the floor.

There were hundreds of humans standing on this plain, and it looked like twice that number had left those boxes with more dropping out. It took seconds for that writhing mass to reach the first humans. They immediately burrowed into the ankles of the first humans.

"Keep still and don't make a single noise," she hissed.

As the worms spread through the human incubators, Walish Din spotted additional movement at the edges. Sure enough, several orange dragons were now running towards the humans, closely followed by double the number of blue natives. They all pushed through the large armour-plated monsters, oblivious to the danger posed by the guardians of the humans.

Not one of those orange dragons raised their staff weapons. They obviously dare not fire those vile, flesh-melting weapons so close to the humans. The blue native rushed through the human statues and literally dived into the worm masses, flying their arms out and trying to funnel the worms towards their mouths.

The orange dragons thundered after them but astonishingly, the monsters didn't try to stop the natives; instead, they all made their way straight towards the girl's cargo ship.

"They're coming for us," she hissed. "They're going to turn us and my ship into molten slush!"

# CHAPTER THIRTEEN

A few moments after the Chaplain's shocking announcement, he had approached Cole and asked him how he felt. Danny had told him that the Chaplain had no other option and had no antagonistic feelings over the man's decision.

Could the man tell that Cole really wanted to throw him out of the airlock? In fact, at this moment, while watching the other humans in this living ship, he wanted to space every single one of them. His hatred towards them didn't stop at the humans either. Cladinus, his so-called friend, stood at the back of the room, silently watching them discuss his fate. Not once had the Gizanti offered a valid reason as to why they shouldn't obey their Imperial orders. He just stood there, not moving and observing.

His imaginary self hadn't shut up about hidden agendas, and right now, Cole felt that the Chaplain, Cladinus, the forces of the God-Emperor, and all the others had tied thick wire around his limbs and we're all pulling him in different directions.

It made him wonder how that man who had Cole's life in the palms of his hands would have chosen if Cole hadn't had his latest vision right in front of them. It seemed incredibly coincidental to experience another vision right at the time when the fate of his life hung in the balance. Could another, unknown force be at work here? Cole shook his head. Why not? Let's add another somebody's hidden agenda to the list. He had a spare wire and they could always tie the end to his nose.

They would alter course, but not for the shipyards. It didn't matter how much hot air and Imperial doctrine spewed from

Trooper Magnus's slimy mouth, the Gizanti would ask the ship to speed towards the birthing planet that he saw in his vision.

He turned away and walked back into the drive room and sat in one of the human-made chairs. They could all argue until they ran out of breath for all he cared.

"Try not to allow their confusion of allegiance to upset you, Danny. Remember, your fellow shipmates are fighting against Imperial brainwashing. I'm surprised that you're still breathing. They could have killed you as soon as the Chaplain announced the change in the orders."

His voice of reason leaned against the wall opposite him, seemingly oblivious to the wet, crimson goo now sliding down the front of his tunic.

"The Empire have had thousands of years to perfect their techniques in order to stop their own from rebelling and bringing upon a much-needed revolution. How apt for the cracks to widen due to their own short-sightedness."

"So how does your theory explain me? I don't feel in any way brainwashed."

"You are special, Danny. You've known this all your life."

His voice of reason walked up to one of the sleep-pods and brushed the tips of his fingers along the outer case. Cole watched in fascination as the red slime dripped off the man's tunic splattered onto the floor and promptly vanished.

"There's nothing special about me," he replied.

"Believe it or not, we are both right. You see, you are not all that special. Hundreds like you are born around the Empire every year. Despite the Imperial geneticists meddling with the human base code, and switching off the areas which encourages such traits as free will, defiance, and creativity, a few are still born which, if not caught, have the potential to become a real pain in the Empire's side once they get older." His voice of reason laughed. "You, my friend, are the only one in thousands of years who slipped through the net. You alone were not diagnosed with these deviant attributes and thrown into the incinerator. It's what separates you from the trillions of other members of your species, Danny Cole. Ironically enough, it's also the reason why you became the best ever squad leader the Empire ever had."

"Oh? Then why are those men still thinking about tossing me out of the airlock? That doesn't exactly tell me that I've won their hearts and minds."

"Did you expect any different? You have not commanded your squad on a single mission yet. Believe me. After a couple of planetary drops, those men would die for you."

Why didn't the alien wake his new squad when they landed on old Earth? If what his voice of reason had said was true, then that alone could have stopped them from potentially endangering his life. Another hidden agenda?

"Who is responsible for all of this? For a start, there's no way that you are just a figment of my imagination, meaning that you are some outside force. Also, why have I suddenly started sharing visions with the God-Emperor? The Chaplain has even hinted that my visions are so much more defined, more detailed." Cole walked up to his voice of reason and placed his hand on Mr. Smith's shoulders. It worried him slightly that he felt very solid under his fingers.

"Walish Din believes that you are all caught in a vast cosmic web, created by some unnamed God. I suppose that a good enough answer."

"Was he the alien I saw in my vision?"

"Yes. His race is called the Diannin. There are a gentle species who keep to themselves. The Empire have known about them for hundreds of years, and yet they have managed to live through two Imperial purges when they expanded their territory. This was either by luck or," his voice of reason winked, "perhaps by design?"

Before he could respond, Mr. Smith did his annoying vanishing act, leaving Cole genuinely alone. He walked back over to the human built seat and sat down, feeling very tired. He still had little idea of what was going on.

Cole took his mind back the events which dominated his last vision. More of one event, really. That was watching the alien and the human female running away from those Gizanti warriors. He witnessed the power of those weapons carried by the huge orange monsters and understood why the Empire was so afraid. There was no defence against a weapon like that. He watched two of them aim and fire at a grounded cargo ship. The blasts turned it into a lump of fused metal. No hand-held device he knew of could release such a huge amount of energy in one burst. Only Imperial warships possessed that capability.

He guessed that the cargo-ship wasn't the primary target. That dubious honour went to the girl and her alien companion. The pair had dived out of the way seconds before the huge aliens had opened fire.

They ran through dozens of human bodies in a desperate attempt to escape the Gizanti pursuers. Cole ran with them, listening to their panting. He needed to know what was happening. Why did none of these humans respond as they pushed past them? How did they all get here and where were they? It also occurred to Cole that somewhere inside him, he probably knew the answers to some of the questions if only he could remember his earlier visions.

Cole could not pose the questions to these two as he was just a passenger; he had no control over this body. He ran just behind the furry alien, stepping where he stepped, and looking at whatever caught Walish Din's attention. He felt like the alien's shadow. Walish Din glanced over his shoulder, worry and concern etched across his face. It didn't surprise Cole to find that he had no problem in understanding the alien's facial expressions. "We're almost through!"

That wasn't directed at him. He found his head turning around. The girl smiled.

"There's a trench a few metres to the left. Head towards it. The one will take us to the nearest settlement."

It struck Cole just how connected he had felt while he'd been running with the girl and the Diannin. Despite not even meeting them, they felt like the family he'd never had. He certainly felt closer to them than this motley bunch in here.

The girl was very beautiful. He wanted to know more about her, especially how she ended up in the company of the furry alien. Cole sighed. "Instead of me."

Cole stood up when the Chaplain entered the room. He turned his back on the man and wrapped his fingers around the chair's armrests. It was the only thing he could think of to stop himself to punching the man. He feared that if he swung at the Chaplain, he wouldn't be able to stop until he'd killed him.

"Trooper Cole, I thought you should be the first one to know that the God has decreed that we are now officially classed as major heretics and consequently, every space-worthy Imperial vessel will be trying to vaporise us."

"So I'm Trooper Cole again? That's nice," he remarked sarcastically. "Does this mean that the men still consider me their squad leader, or are they still deciding whether to throw me out of the airlock?" Cole gripped the armrests even tighter. "It's okay, Chaplain. Take your time in answering, I have all day."

He received no reply. Not that he expected one. The Chaplain was too much of a coward for that. Cole waited for another minute before turning around. The man had left him, probably skulked back into his own room. He uncurled his fingers and straightened his back before turning around. Sure enough, the man had left him alone.

Did this mean that he'd soon be able test out Mr. Smith's cute little theory of his 'men' dying for Cole after one mission? It would be funny if it wasn't tragic as well as potentially hazardous to his and the health of the ones they're supposed to be rescuing.

Cole paused. He had no clue if this ship was actually heading for the planet where his two companions were fighting the altered Gizanti. All his comment meant was that this ship wasn't heading for the shipyards. He hurried towards the hatchway, intending to force the full message from the Chaplain when Cladinus blocked his path.

"Do not be concerned with the Chaplain," he said. "You will be joining up with your companions shortly."

"How did you...? No, don't bother replying." Cole looked back to the sleep-pods. "So shouldn't we start to make preparations for sleep-suppression?"

This news gave him a cause to celebrate. It meant that he'd be able to put his real talents to use, instead of not knowing and second guessing his way through the metaphysical shit that had taken up permanent residence in his life. As for the other men, the ones who had the audacity to suggest that they spaced him a short while ago, they will soon understand what it was like to be under the command of a proper squad leader. Once they were all out of sleep-suppression, he fully intended to put those bastards through utter hell.

"We will be entering the star system very soon, Danny. I suggest you make preparations."

"How is that possible? Surely, this ship isn't that fast!"

The Gizanti shook his head. "No coordinates were decided right after we left the planet of your ancestors, Danny."

"Before we even knew about the girl and the other furry alien? Why does that not even surprise me anymore? I take it that the Chaplain wasn't aware that you had no intention of going to the Terran shipyards?"

The Gizanti shrugged. "We are just here to transport you and your fellow humans to wherever you desire," he replied. The alien turned around.

"Wait, before you go, Cladinus, just tell me one thing."

He looked back at Danny. "The answer is yes. We do know who is helping you, Walish Din, and Jessica."

After the large alien dropped the bombshell which Danny had already suspected, Cladinus stepped back. He took hold of Cole's shoulders and gently propelled him over to the other humans who had assembled in the next room.

"Cladinus, you had better see this," said the Chaplain. "I think we have a bit of a problem." He rushed over to the largest monitor in the drive room. "You had better be right about right about this ship's capabilities. If you were just boasting, then we're all dead!"

The split screen showed hundreds of small vessels in four rows fleeing the system, guarded by eight Imperial warships, two destroyers, and a dreadnought. As Cole watched, the dreadnought, both destroyers, and three warships broke off and headed towards their ship.

"We're all dead!" said Trooper Magnus while glaring at Cole.

The other half of the monitor screen showed Cole what awaited them beyond the Imperial ships. The invading aliens had created a vast energy matrix around the planet. Hundreds of captured space vehicles anchored the pulsating beams. The technology involved in creating such a divine sight in such a short time boggles the mind.

Cole wanted to join Magnus in his pathetic bleating. Their plight really did look impossible.

"Sergeant Cole, please get your men ready," said the Chaplain quietly.

So now he had a field promotion. Why did he not feel all that honoured? Cole switched his attention to the other side of the monitor. The approaching Imperial dreadnought was almost within firing range. He suspected that this was going to be the shortest field promotion in the history of humankind.

"Have you gone blind?" screamed Magnus. "Just look at the monitor, you big orange bastard! They're going to atomise us at any second."

Cladinus waved his large hand across the glowing panel next to him. "They are of no concern," he said.

The eight Imperial warships suddenly halted their course and turned until their bows now faced the alien ships. With all their weapons at the front, each warship could be taken out with the minimum of effort. Cole watched the men, each one looking as confused as each other. They must know that the Gizanti ship had done this, that this little spacecraft had the capability to render some of the most advanced pieces of human-built space vessels utterly useless. The Chaplain wasn't confused; if anything, he appeared to be enjoying the spectacle.

Now Cladinus turned his attention to the pride of the Imperial navy. The dreadnought was the most powerful weapon of war ever built. There were only two in existence. This behemoth, larger than all the other warships put together, had purged entire planetary populations of Imperial-hating alien deviants. Nothing in the galactic expanse could match it for superior firepower.

Cole looked at the other side of the screen at the energy grid around the planet, and he just knew that if that huge ship had drifted a little closer to the planet, then it too would now be part of that matrix, and there would have been nothing in its extensive armoury that would have helped it. That dreadnought was now heading straight for the destroyer, with all its gun ports open.

"Sergeant, we do not have much time."

Cole nodded at the Chaplain before striding over to the assembled soldiers. He stopped directly in front of Magnus. "Are you a coward, marine?"

The man glared at him. "I don't care who you are. Nobody calls me a coward and lives to tell the tale."

He held up a single finger. "This is the number of marines in the whole Imperial Navy who answered yes to that question." Cole then clasped the marine's shoulders. "You are outspoken. You are not afraid to voice your opinion." He looked over at the monitor. "Even if your opinion does transpire to be wrong. You are not a coward, Magnus, just a hot-headed idiot."

The other marines chuckled under their breath.

Cole turned his attention to them. "In my opinion, you are all idiots. None of you are worth the uniform you wear. I don't believe that any of you would last more than a few minutes under real battlefield conditions." Cole pointed at the planet. "That is what we are about to face. The enemy has weapons which make anything we possess look like children's toys." He then took two steps back. "Are any of you prepared to die for a cause which for once in our lives is worth dying for?" He took a deep breath. "Are you prepared to show that I'm wrong about your abilities?"

"Follow me, please," said the Chaplain.

When the drive room was clear of everyone but Cole and the Gizanti, the huge alien approached him. "This will be a simple rescue mission," he said. "The Battle Sister knows the coordinates to the two other chosen ones and will attempt to place you and your men nearby."

"Wait, okay, you've shown that this ship has outmatched anything the Empire has in their arsenal, but exactly how are you going to get us to the surface? Surely you're not thinking of ramming this ship into that energy grid?"

"No. Even this mighty Battle Sister could not penetrate that. No ship could."

"So how do you intend to get us down?"

"In the same manner as the invading aliens. The grid stops solid matter from reaching the surface; nothing else. Otherwise, how would they release the devices growing inside those incubators?"

It took him a moment for Cole to grasp that concept. "Are you telling me that your species has the ability to displace matter?"

Cladinus nodded.

"I don't believe it. Once again, you have managed to shock me. I take it that the Empire is not aware of this?"

"If you shared the Galactic Expanse with an aggressive, xenophobic, territorial alien, would you not keep quiet?" Cladinus smiled. "I wish you all good luck."

"Are you not coming?"

He shook his head. "No, I cannot leave the Battle Sister. It will not take the humans commanding those Imperial ships to realise the sleights we cast over their controls. You had best attend to your men. It could take you some time to persuade the other humans to pick up the Gizanti weapons which the Battle Sister has graciously allowed you to operate."

"Will that not be dangerous for you, Cladinus? You said that the weapons will deplete your energy."

The large alien gave the best approximation to a human shrug.

"I believe that the Battle Sister should be able to protect me, my friend." He released a long sigh. "I am hoping that the guns will steal the life-energy from the alerted Gizanti, which should help you and your men put them out of their torment."

Cole couldn't imagine Cladinus' own torment at giving aliens a cache of weapons in order to kill members of his own race.

"You should pray that this is the case; otherwise, our weapons will be useless and you already know that human-made weapons will not stop them."

Cole took his hand. "I will do everything in my power to ensure the safety of the two we're here to extract."

# CHAPTER FOURTEEN

Walish Din opened the tiny Hessian sack and peered inside. There didn't appear to be any change in its appearance. He took that as a good sign, considering he didn't even know what they did. He wrapped his fingers around the top of the sack before joining the girl by the front of the burnt-out shop. For some reason, the sight of the thing in the sack totally freaked her out. In his view, her behaviour was so unjustified. If it hadn't been for his innovative quick thinking, both of them would still be back on that sandy plain, fused with what was left of the girl's cargo ship.

"Why don't you leave that thing here?" said the girl. She shivered violently. "I still can't believe you did that, Walish Din."

He couldn't quite believe it either. "It saved our lives. They dared not fire, even when we cleared the incubators. That thing is the reason why we are still breathing."

"Yeah, well. That situation will soon change if we do not keep moving. The monsters won't be far behind us."

Walish Din silently agreed with her yet kept hold of his prize while staying close to the girl as she threaded her way through the settlement's narrow streets. He hoped she knew where to go as the Diannin could not tell one street from the next one. They all looked the same; just a single rectangle hole cut into each pale-blue, featureless dwelling. He slowed down and peered inside one of the darkened buildings to discover three pairs of oval yellow eyes staring back at him.

He caught up with the girl while listening to the occasional weapon blasts in the distance. They were becoming less often now. He figured that there couldn't be much resistance left. It also meant that they wouldn't be that much life left either. The orange dragons were not exactly a forgiving bunch.

"These dwellings are occupied."

"I know that," she replied. The girl stopped walking and turned to face him. She looked at the bag and grimaced before staring at him. "When was the last time you happened to glance into the sky?"

"What's the point? All there is up there is whatever the aliens are building."

"I thought you would have felt it by now, Walish Din."

"Felt what?"

She sighed. "It must be because of that vile thing you refuse to leave behind. He's coming, the last one, the third member is already in this system!"

Her eyes were shining with excitement. Walish Din hadn't felt anything but terror, and yet he could not doubt her conviction. "We're being rescued?"

"I'm sure of it," she replied. "We just need to make sure we're as far away from the altered Gizanti as possible. Which is why you need to get rid of that right now."

He gripped the sack even tighter. There's no way he could get rid of this; it was the only thing that kept them alive. Walish Din just couldn't understand why she didn't see this. They would not have made it through the human incubators with this. Walish Din had done something which totally went against every Diannin instinct. He had stopped running, stood directly in front of the closest human, and punched his fist into the human's stomach cavity. His hand easily passed through the thin wall. He had wanted to scream, pull his arm out of there, and find a very dark corner to hide, but he persevered, pushing his fist through all that freezing jelly-like substance until his probing fingers finally located one of the small pods growing inside there.

"They won't fire at us while I carry this."

"Look around you, Walish Din! It's true, they won't fire at us, but it won't stop them from attacking all these poor people. Thanks to your short-sightedness, you've put all these innocent people in terrible danger. You need to…"

Her voice died away at the sound of another alien weapon blast. This wasn't a distant sound; it came from where they had just been. It originated from just a few metres behind them. They were here already!

Walish Din felt sick. She was right. The orange dragons would kill everybody in this settlement to get to them. They had to find some way of leading the monsters out of here! He turned around and started to walk towards the sound of the alien staff weapon blast.

"Come back, Walish Din. They'll kill you!"

That was a possibility, but he didn't think that would happen while he still held the sack. Besides, the Diannin hadn't forgotten that he'd been able to move them out of the way when he first met the girl. Perhaps they'll do the same?

He ground his teeth in annoyance when he heard her running after him. Three orange dragons had already seen him approach and were already thundering towards him. Walish Din held up the bag and willed them to stand aside, just like before.

Nothing happened; the monsters kept running at Walish Din.

"You should have stayed away," he muttered. "Now we're both going to die!"

"No, we're not," she said, reaching up and snatching the sack out of his hand.

She threw it to the side of them. Two of the dragons immediately turned towards the sack, leaving the last one staring straight at them. The girl grabbed his arm before running straight towards the dragon. Just as it reached out to grab them, the girl threw something in its face.

For the first time since encountering these hateful creatures, Walish Din heard one of them make a sound. He glanced over his head and saw the dragon rolling about on the floor, shrieking.

"I still had my worm samples left," she said.

Just before she pulled him out of sight, he saw dozens of blue natives rushing out of their dwellings, diving onto the orange dragon. They no longer looked like the harmless, fearful creatures. They were literally ripping open the creature's face in a desperate attempt to reach those few worms.

The girl pulled him inside one of the empty dwellings and dropped him onto the floor. "Stay there and don't make a noise." She then crawled on her knees over to the entrance way. The Diannin leaned against the wall and gazed into the darkness, studying the vague shapes of what he guessed was furniture. He heard a couple more energy blasts before the only sound he could hear was his own heavy breathing.

He looked over at the girl and wished she would come over here and sit with him, perhaps even hold him tight. That would be nice. It might even help combat the dreadful feeling of imminent death that had now returned.

The girl was right about sensing the closeness of the remaining person. Now that the sack containing that alien device was no longer with him, he too felt his presence. He knew that this must mean that whatever path that the deity had dropped him on must now be reaching the end, and yet Walish Din couldn't help but feel that they had abandoned both him and the girl. How else could he account for the fact that right when he needed them, the bastards took away the one thing that could have saved them?

What about the girl? Had she lost her power too? He sighed. It's not like they would be able to check until it was too late. If he found himself wandering across the Plains of Gopin the next time one of those orange dragons aimed and fired at them, he would know he was right.

This did not exactly help to console him.

"Are you okay, Walish Din?"

He nodded, then realised that it was too dark in here for her to see that. "Yes," he whispered. "I am unharmed."

"I can feel him, Walish Din. He's here. He is on the planet."

He noticed the change too, but unlike her, the Diannin wasn't as confident about voicing his feelings. "How can that be possible?"

He didn't immediately answer him. "Are you okay?"

"No, I don't think I am."

"It is them out there? Please tell me that they have gone."

"No. Three more monsters have just arrived." She yelped. "Oh no! Make that four."

The girl turned around. Even in the dim light, he saw the terror etched on her face. She scrambled away from the opening and wrapped her arms around his body. Through three layers of clothing, the girl's heart still thudded against his chest. Walish Din then pressed his mouth hard against her shoulder to stop the scream when an orange dragon's huge head pushed through the opening.

\*\*\*\*

His four men seemed to be adapting to this situation far better than Cole had anticipated. Perhaps they might actually survive the unknown challenges facing them on this unknown planet. He found himself unconsciously stroking the Gizanti gun stock again. He would have to stop doing that. To think that he thought that persuading his men to accept the guns without protest would be his greatest challenge. Obviously not so; not by the way they were holding them. Did the men even realise they were all holding their new weapons like they would a new lover? Was there something insidious within the weapon which forced the holder to bond with it? From what he had already seen and learned from the Gizanti, that possibility was very real. Still, did it really matter as long as the revolting-looking guns performed their allotted tasks?

"Magnus, Livingston, cover our exit and stay on point. I need to know the second something changes. Is that clear?"

The men nodded before following Livingston to the open gates. It pleased him to see that the pair of them were keeping their heads below the wall height to minimize the chances of being seen by the enemy. He was playing on the hope that as long as the big orange bastards didn't see or hear him of his men then they won't start shooting.

"You two, follow me." He followed the example of the others by staying low while he raced out of the courtyard.

He reached the next building and flattened his back against the blue featureless wall. The remaining soldiers took up position at either side. He put up his arm and made a fist before bringing it back down. Both Magnus and Livingston looked nonplussed at his bizarre behaviour. Cole ground his teeth in annoyance. What kind of marine does not understand basic hand signals? "You two move forward," he hissed, "and keep your eyes on the landscape."

He waited for the men to move past before turning to the marine on his right. "Has the nausea left you yet?"

The young man nodded. "Yeah, thanks. I feel a little better now, Sergeant," he replied. "I think the fresh air has helped to shift it." Private Dave Jeffery's mouth split open into a wide grin. "That was some ride though." He paused. "Although I am not sure that I want to repeat it any time soon."

They believed that the ship would be blasting their way through that orbital matrix. It was such an easy mistake to make, especially after witnessing the ease at which that had stopped the Imperial ships. It is what Cole would have believed if he hadn't known any better.

His voice of reason had suggested giving them time to adapt to their new situation, and judging from their initial disgust when first seeing the alien weapons, Cole knew that his trepidation was valid. Even as the Chaplain led them onto the displacement pads, he said that it was just a decontamination booth.

Their combined screaming while the ship de-constructed their bodies atom by atom would likely stay with him for a long time. Cole knew he screamed too. It felt like the alien ship was eating him alive. The next thing he remembered was opening his eyes, covered in sweat, and shaking like a leaf. The air which filled his lungs tasted strange, and the light filtering through that alien construction hurt his eyes at first.

It had taken him a minute or two for all of his senses to re-align. Once his bearings returned, Cole had set about ensuring the other four were okay. While checking the marines, he had wondered why it hadn't affected him so badly. The ordeal quickly faded and, thankfully, left no scars, mental or physical. He remembered the Chaplain privately mentioning that the ship had assured him that she had not detected any movement anywhere near the landing site. Doing his hardest not to show the Chaplain how much this unknown procedure was worrying him, he had simply said that it wasn't the first time that he had led a squad into a sudden firefight.

If the unit had materialised in the midst of those orange monsters, they would not have stood a chance. They would have melted every one of his men while they were as helpless as newborn babies.

Cole considered the young marine's concern. Would their return journey be as traumatic? As worries went, it wasn't exactly at the top of Cole's list. They had to complete the impossible before he even considered contacting the Chaplain.

"We have a sighting."

Cole hoped it was the two they were supposed to extract. The Gizanti ship had assured him that she would place the five of them as close as she dare to their location. He watched Magnus adjust his bio-scanner and impatiently waited for the man to confirm his hope.

"I do not know what they are," he said, not taking his gaze away. "They are not Imperial citizens. Blue skin tone, a slender body mass, and about a metre taller than the average human." The man dropped his bio-scanner and raised the weapon.

"Stand down, Magnus!" he hissed. "Stand down!"

"That's the indigenous population."

"They look suspicious. Probably spies for the enemy; at best, they'll be collaborators."

"The only lifeforms around here acting suspiciously is us. An aggressive alien species had invaded their world. They are most likely running in fear, looking for somewhere to hide. Magnus, focus on our primary mission and locate our targets."

He sensed movement and spun around to find private Jeffery getting to his feet. "Get back down, you fool, what are you playing at?" The man had already left his position. Cole jumped up and ran towards him then skidded to a complete halt at the sight of a huge armour-plated orange monster staring straight at Private Jeffery.

"Cladinus," said Jeffery. "I thought you were staying on the ship."

"Move out of the way," yelled Cole, raising his weapon. "That's not him."

He dared not shoot in case his blast hit the young man, but the altered Gizanti had no such objection. It fired once. A bright blue flame enveloped Jeffery's left leg, eating through skin, flesh, and bone within seconds. The shrieking man fell to the floor. Once he was down, the other three marines opened fire. The strange energies bursting from the alien weapons turned the huge creature into a pool of bright red slush.

Both Livingston and Magnus dropped to their knees to try and do what they could for their fallen comrade. Cole sensed movement to his left and grabbed the pair of them by the backs of their jackets, dragging the men out of the way before he turned his own weapon to the side and fired one shot.

The stream of energy smashed into the outside courtyard wall, missing his intended target by inches. He dropped to the floor and rolled to the side as a second altered Gizanti warrior fired its staff weapon. The blast hit the moaning soldier full on, dissolving him instantly. Cole fired again. This time, he hit it in the face. The huge creature toppled against the melted stone.

"Where had they come from?" screamed Magnus. "The view was clear, I know it was. There wasn't anything larger than those blue things moving about."

This was all his fault. Cole should have paid more attention. Now, thanks to him, one of his men was now gone. He would not lose another one. "The dwellings," he said. "They were hiding in the dwellings." Cole smacked the butt of his gun against Livingston's shoulder. "They came from in there," he hissed, pointing at the closest building. "Go check it out." He took shelter against the closest wall and scanned the visible area. He prayed that they had not just walked into an ambush. If that was indeed the case, then they would not last much longer. Those large monsters could be hiding in any of the dozens of buildings in this settlement.

He was also now very aware that they had made their presence known. Even if the monsters were not waiting for them, the bastards would know they were here now. He looked up when Livingston staggered outside. The soldier leaned over and vomited.

"Are you okay?" Magnus ran over to his buddy, but the other soldier waved him away.

"I am uninjured. The contents of that dwelling are not a pleasant sight." He wiped the back of his hand across his mouth before running over to Cole. "There are alien bodies stacked neatly against three walls. There is also evidence that suggests those things we melted were dining on them." He took a deep breath. "There is also what looks like a tunnel leading from the building."

A thin stream of fluid, leaking from the Gizanti's liquefied remains, flowed into what had once been Dave Jeffery. Cole stared as the two colours, each from the different species, intermixed. Such a beautiful pattern. He tore his gaze away. "You saw no other Gizanti?"

"No, just the corpses."

"Then our route is decided. We'll use the tunnels."

"I'm not going back in there. No way."

"You'll do as the sergeant ordered," replied Magnus.

That surprised him. Cole expected Magnus to side with Livingston. He faced the remaining soldier. "Davis, are you okay, son? You haven't spoken a single word since we arrived on this planet."

"When you grabbed me, Sergeant, back on that other planet, I honestly believed that you would kill me. I had never been so scared in my life." He swallowed hard. "That is, until I lost my best friend, Dave." He looked straight at Livingston. A single tear rolled down the young man's cheek. "I remember when you continually raged at the other units in the palace. The ones who were sent on the important missions, the ones who always had the best equipment. The ones who were never ridiculed." He turned to Cole. "Livingston, they told us when Cole was delivered to us that this man here once commanded the most effective assassination unit in the Empire. Livingston, this man here has just saved our lives. If it hadn't been for his lightning reflexes just now, we all would dead."

Both Magnus and Livingston had bowed their heads now.

"That fear had never left me," continued Davis. "But I am getting better at controlling it." He finally raised his head. "Thanks to our new sergeant." The walked pushed past Livingston and strode right up to the open doorway. He then turned his head. "Remember your training, what little we had. Look at our location." He pointed to the next dwelling. "There could be some of those armoured monsters in there, Livingston. Just waiting for you to pass them. Maybe there are some in the next dwelling, or the one after that. The odds are stacked against us, and as the only marine here who's had experience with street fighting, I'll follow what Cole says."

He waited until the remaining marines followed Davis inside before taking up position at the rear. Cole had stayed silent during the young man's little speech, deciding that it was for the best if Davis said what had been troubling him. Cole knew that no other squad leader would have let the boy ramble on; they would have either whipped him or shot him. These were extraordinary times and his three remaining men were not ordinary soldiers. He might as well be commanding civilians.

It is what the other Imperial soldiers thought they were.

He stopped walking as soon as he entered the building and looked at every wall. There was no sign of any corpses. Granted, a few gnawed bones shared the dusty floor with a few small stones, but he saw nothing to indicate that any body had been stored here. A chemical odour hung in the air. He wrinkled his nose. It was an odd smell but not altogether too unpleasant. It certainly wasn't the stench of dead meat.

"They were here," cried Livingston. "I did not make any of it up." He stormed over to one of the walls. "This was piled high with them."

"It does not matter," replied Cole. He saw that at least Livingston had not been wrong about the alternate exit. The other two were close now; they were almost at their location. "If this was a storage facility, then it stands to reason that it does get emptied." Cole picked up one of the bones. "The two creatures could either be bringing more food here or were guarding it."

"Yes, but where did it go?"

Magnus grinned at Livingston. "If it even existed."

Cole sighed heavily. "It's suspect that it went in the same way we arrived. Now, shall we continue with our mission or perhaps you would prefer to wait here until more monsters arrive?" He hurried over to the grate in the floor and slid it back. He took a glowglobe from his belt, twisted it, then threw it down. The white light coming from the device showed his hard-packed soil and nothing else. He suspected that the monsters didn't even know it was here. This is where his instincts were telling him to go. This tunnel would lead them straight to the two.

He dropped into the hole, picked up the glowglobe, and threw it further into the tunnel. The light showed him more hard-packed soil and nothing else. Cole looked down to check for footprints. The only ones he saw were his own. He moved further into the tunnel to allow the others to drop down. That chemical smell had followed him down here as well. Cole shook his head. He had better things to think about. It was likely coming from the earth.

Cole activated his last glowglobe and held it next to the weapon as he slowly traversed along the tunnel. Before long, the tunnel bifurcated. He stopped walking and peered into the darkness. His instinct suggested that this route would not take him and his men to where they needed to go, so he carried on.

"Sergeant, I don't think we should go this way," hissed Livingston. "It doesn't feel right."

Magnus chuckled. "Coward."

"Shut up, I am not a coward. I am just saying. Can you not feel the difference?"

Cole stopped again. He lifted his head, closed his eyes, and tuned out their voices. That irresistible pull could not be denied. This was the closest route to the other two. He knew this as sure as he knew his own name.

Yet despite the total faith in that feeling, he could not just disregard the marine's warning. For a start, Livingston had no reason to lie about the bodies he saw, and his theory about them displacing the bodies had been gnawing at him ever since he had started moving along this tunnel. "I want you all to stay silent and keep focused on…"

Several rocks the size of their head pushed through both walls and landed in their midst. That chemical stench blasted out of the gaping holes left from the displaced rocks. "Back!" ordered Cole. "Move back to the other tunnel."

He waited until the men were out of the way before he dropped to one knee. He lifted his gun, aimed it at the nearest wall exit, and impatiently waited for whatever was crawling along that hole. Again, Cole wanted to scream for not looking at the evidence. The answers were there, right in front of his eyes. Those aliens hadn't removed them, why would they?

He heard the sound of shifting soil, yet the noise wasn't coming from any of those exits. Cole jumped to his feet and staggered back. Oh no, the bastards were beneath their feet! He ran backwards then stopped just before he smacked into the other three.

"They're behind us too!" said Davis. "They're everywhere!"

"Quiet!" snapped Cole. He let off a single blast at the tunnel floor. The ground directly under his feet heated up, almost to the point of melting his boot before dissipating. He fired again, this time at the wall. "On my order, you follow me." Cole aimed at the opposite wall and fired again. "Run!"

Human-like screams erupted from all around them as they raced along the now-fused tunnel. Cole heard more movement and felt the soil beneath his boots shifting. There was only one direction left. He aimed his weapon up and fired a continuous blast into the ceiling.

More screams joined the already deafening chorus; this time, the voices were from his men. He turned around and dragged them down. It wasn't dirt above their heads! Scraps of burning fabric rained down on the four soldiers. Cole grabbed Magnus and rolled him over before he slammed his own back against the wall.

Cole blinked as the bright sunlight stabbed his eyes. "Oh fuck!"

This wasn't a damn tunnel, it was a trench, and they now found themselves totally surrounded by hundreds of altered Gizanti warriors and every single one of them were now aiming their staff weapons at him and the three marines.

"No! I will not allow this to happen."

There she was. The pair of them, surrounded by these huge orange monsters. The girl flew out her arms just as the first volley of superheated energy left those staff weapons. Cole staggered backwards and threw both arms over his head.

"How are we still alive?" cried Davis.

The alien monsters continued to fire their staffs, but an invisible umbrella surrounding the four soldiers deflected their blasts down and into the ground, turning the affected area into a narrow moat of bubbling lava.

They never stopped firing at them. Cole had to cover his eyes to protect against the intense light. None of the heat penetrated that barrier. He slowly got to his feet, listening to talk of witchcraft and sorcery coming from Magnus. Through gaps in the energy slamming into the barrier, he saw the girl lift her companion to his feet. The little alien screamed something in an unknown language before he too threw out his arms.

Every staff weapon flew out of their hands before the monsters themselves were swept up into the air. The little alien continued to chant while the Gizanti warriors swirled around like uprooted trees in a tornado. The little alien's voice suddenly went dead. Every Gizanti dropped into the boiling lava.

Cole leaped out of the trench. He stopped to help the others out then looked beyond the glowing moat. Both the human girl and the little alien had collapsed on each other. He moaned in anguish before running towards them, hoping that whatever they had just done had not killed them.

# CHAPTER FIFTEEN

The Chaplain activated the remaining sleep-pod's waking process. He waited for a moment until he saw the occupant stir before joining Cladinus on the bridge. As he walked through the dark red walls which rhythmically pulsated, Philip found himself asking at what moment in journey did this organic vessel feel like home?

The large Gizanti stood beside a monitor screen which covered one of the living bulkheads. The display showed him the planet which he once thought of his home. The Imperial Terran world. The centre of this vast Empire which had ruled the Galactic Expanse for over three thousand years.

They had reached orbit with very little opposition.

"Where are the orbitals?" Surely they had not been destroyed. There should have been eleven huge orbiting stations visible yet he saw nothing.

"Moved," replied the Gizanti. "For safety, to prepare for imminent invasion." Cladinus turned his massive head. "It appears that the God-Emperor does take his visions seriously."

"It made no sense when we first left the weave and it still makes no sense. Is your ship really so unstoppable?" The thousands of Imperial defence drones stationed close to the two outer planets flew on an intercept course towards the ship once it had emerged into real space. They had locked on and fired, and yet every missile had strayed off course.

The four warships that tried to bring them down were now trapped in the gravity well of this system's only gas giant, and before the Gizanti had asked Philip to activate the sleep-pods, the

141

large alien had disabled the planet's twelve weapon's platforms. He had casually remarked that it was not really necessary as they were utterly ineffective against the Battle Sister's shielding. The Chaplain detected just a touch of pride when he had announced that.

"The warships have escaped the gas giant and the defence drones are now fully restored."

He looked at the Gizanti, worried. "I have not expected that. Will they be a threat?"

"The others are stirring, Philip. It is time."

Cladinus left the Chaplin wanting to hit the big orange alien for deliberately not answering his question yet again. He bit his bottom lip and followed him over to the sleep-pods, stopping in-between their two new arrivals. Neither of them had woken before placing them into the pods, and even though Cladinus had told them all not to worry, he still couldn't help but wonder how they were to complete their mission if neither of them opened their eyes.

Cole groaned before he slowly sat up. He pulled out the drips then looked straight at the Chaplain. "Are they okay?" The squad leader climbed out of the pod, wrapped a blanket around his body, then staggered over. Cladinus rushed to the man and grabbed his shoulders.

"Do not excite your body, Danny," said the alien. "The drugs in your system have yet to take effect."

"I don't care about any of that, you damned fool!" he shouted. "Tell me they are going to wake up. Tell me that we still have a chance."

"Do you not know the answer to that question?" replied the Gizanti. He then gazed across at the Chaplain. "Could you please inform your excitable human friend what occurred once we entered this star system?"

"We emerged from the weave close to the outer planets and…"

"That's not possible!" said Cole. "No ship can enter real space in that region; it is too heavily guarded."

Cladinus managed to sit the human down. He then placed his hands on Cole's shoulders. "It was necessary."

"The drones fired and yet every missile missed the ship," continued Philip. "It is not possible to leave the weave so close to the home-world, Sergeant Cole. The God-Emperor does not permit it." The Chaplain remembered Cole and the three men discussing how both the girl and the little alien had saved them. Davis and Livingston went to great lengths describing how the girl was able to stop all those energy blasts with the power of her mind. "Cladinus, are you saying that the girl saved the ship, even though she was in the sleep-pod?"

The alien nodded. "It was necessary," he repeated.

Cladinus walked over to the sleep-pod holding the girl. Cole ran over and stood beside the Gizanti; the man beamed with happiness. Philip saw why. She sat up and looked around the room, only stopping when she saw the little alien staring back at her. Their gazes met and the alien grinned.

"We have little time left," said Cladinus, helping the girl out of the sleep-pod. "It will not be long before the altered mechs reach this system. When that time approaches, it would be optimum for us to have completed the impeachment."

So that was why he felt the need to tell him about the restoration of the system's defences. "What happens if the mechs arrive before we finish?"

Cladinus handed the girl a small capsule and glass of liquid. Once she had taken it, he moved to the little alien. "When the mechs reach this star system, their only goal is to destroy this planet utterly, for it will be the only location in the Galactic Expanse where your species still lives." Cladinus gave the little alien another capsule. "The pods growing inside all those millions of incubators are now mature. Very soon, the aggressors will begin displacing the pods to every planet, moon, orbital, and spacecraft within the galactic expanse. They only have one purpose and that is to eradicate human tissue."

The Chaplain paled as the enormity of their dreadful plight began to sink in.

"Do you wish to continue conversing, Chaplain? I am sure that there are many more fascinating discussions we can have before the pod designated to the Battle Sister appears among us."

\*\*\*

The Chaplain pressed his body hard against the palace wall, trying to stop the uncontrollable shakes from showing. Not that any of the others were watching him. They were all suffering from displacement sickness, with the exception of the two aliens. Both Cladinus and Walish Din looked fine. Cole had mentioned that it wasn't as bad as the last time. He dreaded to think what that could have been like.

Two marines rushed back and crouched behind Cole. Davis pointed north and reported his findings to the sergeant. Philip did not hear a single word of the conversation nor did he wish to. Just the fact that he was here, again, scared him witless without needing to know what the squad leader was planning.

So far, they had encountered very little resistance, but that situation would soon alter once they had reached the inner palace. He watched the three soldiers stand up and run back the way they came.

"What's going on now?" he asked Cole.

The young sergeant came up and patted him on the shoulder. "Don't worry about that. I've sent them to cover our exits." He crouched beside the Chaplain. "Now," he said, smiling. "We've hit a bit of a problem. You see, nobody knows the exact location of the God-Emperor's chamber."

"No, of course not. The way to the chamber is changed on a regular basis." Philip had not stopped reliving his vision once most of the nausea had left him. This place was nothing like the palace that he and the other guards defended from the altered Gizanti. It just did not make any sense.

"The Index could help us, Chaplain. She will be able to plot us a route straight to the God-Emperor's hidden chamber."

"Yes, but the key was lost."

Cladinus pushed a hand under one of his armoured plates. He grunted then pulled out Philip's crystal key.

"I don't believe it," he said once the Gizanti had dropped it into the palm of his hand. "Where did you find it?"

"We can talk about that later," hissed Cole. "Right now, you need to lead us to your –"

144

Three blaster charges slammed into the wall opposite, sending shards of stone out in all directions. The Gizanti managed to cover the cowering humans with his bulk. Cladinus fired back, his human weapon looking so small in the giant alien's hand. The Chaplain pushed through the alien's thick body and joined both the girl and Cole.

"Where are they?" he asked. "I can't see anyone." The Chaplain raised his gun, only for Cole to gently lower his arm.

"They don't matter. Focus on where we are, Chaplain. I need you to take us to your quarters. Can you do that?"

The Chaplain shook his head. "No. We could be on any level, in any area of this complex. Do not look so concerned, Cole. Any terminal will suffice." He slung the weapon over his back. "Come on, follow me. The public terminals are generally in the numerous Halls of Shadows. There is one of those on every level. They are not hard to locate."

He moved past Walish Din and hurried along the narrow stone corridor until the Chaplain reached the first corner. The shakes had left him now. He put that down to feeling that finally he had something to contribute, even if he had been relegated to the position of a lowly tour guide. It did not fit that a man of his position should be sneaking like some thief from the lower orders. He was a man of position, of respect. Someone to be feared.

There was an arched doorway at the end of this corridor. It looked a little too ornate to lead to some cupboard. He smiled to himself. Could he be so lucky to find this level's Hall of Shadows so easily?

He saw the door begin to open. The Gizanti grabbed him and dragged the man back into the shadows. The low recharge whine coming from their SS80 assault pistols covered the sound of running feet coming towards them.

"Stay down!" hissed Cole.

They were preparing to gun down whoever passed them!

He pushed the alien's huge hand off him and moved into their path.

"Get back here, you idiot," hissed the girl.

Four young men almost ran into him. "Stop!" he growled. It did not surprise Philip to find that he had just bumped into the soldiers that he had seen in his vision. "Do you know who I am?"

The sergeant at arms nodded. "Yeah, I do." He raised his weapon. "You're one of the arch traitors."

"Incorrect. I am Philip Diocolis, Prime Chaplain of the Third Imperial Order. Those commands you received were a fabrication, a falsehood sent from the very abominations which you and your brave soldiers are about to face." The Chaplain clicked his fingers twice. "You are to escort myself and my associates to God-Emperor's revered Inner Sanctum." He pulled out the Index. "I have crucial news which could very well stop our glorious Empire from being crushed by the deviants which seek to destroy us."

He could see the indecision fighting across the poor man's features. The Chaplain just hoped that the urge to obey would win through. If not, then these men would not be able to repeat what they had just witnessed. Philip's associates would see to that.

The Chaplain leaned forward until he was an inch away from the sergeant at arms. "You once told me that you wanted to live to return to your beautiful wife, Sergeant."

The man hurriedly stepped away. "You cannot know that!"

Philip smiled benevolently. "Do you believe in prophecy?"

"The God-Emperor wills that we do, for it is the visions which protect us."

"I have seen the prophecies," he said, "and in one I saw you and your troops die a needless death. In that vision, the Empire and every human in the Galactic Expanse died. Do you wish for that to happen?" Philip turned and gestured the others to show themselves. As soon as they saw the sight of the huge Gizanti warrior, they all raised their weapons. The Chaplain stood in front of the nearest guard. He placed his hand over the barrel and pushed it down. "Do not fear, Trooper Delaney. These soldiers perform the will of the God-Emperor too."

For several seconds, nobody spoke. The Chaplain prayed that his associates would keep their heads. He also prayed that the palace guards would heed his message. If any of them began to fire, it would be a bloodbath.

Somewhere within the palace walls, the sound of boosters racing down the stone floors really he'd him. If he didn't do something right now, then the addition of more palace guards certainly would be the end of all of them. The Chaplain took one step forward and opened his mouth just as the wall a few inches above their heads literally melted.

"The invaders have already breached the palace!" cried Cole.

The Chaplain shook his head in disbelief. "How can that be?"

"It is probable that they were here before we arrived," replied Cladinus.

Two more blasts turned more of the wall area into molten slag. Philip threw himself at Trooper Delaney just as another blast blew out the door. "That is your enemy, Sergeant! Now do as you're ordered and take us to the inner sanctum!"

The man nodded once before scrambling to hides feet. "This way," he gasped, taking the lead.

Philip stayed with the sergeant at arms as they ran through the palace. They found no other humans as they ran from room to room, an observation that the Chaplain could not believe. Had they really evacuated the whole palace? If so, then the God-Emperor must truly believe team visions. The Chaplain was not sure whether he thought this was a good or bad thing.

"Did you really see me in a vision?"

"Yes," he replied. "You died an honourable death."

The sergeant at arms stopped. He suddenly turned and grabbed the Chaplain. "My life means nothing, but will you see that my wife is cared for?"

"I swear on my robe." The Chaplain gently removed the man's arms. He scanned the area and realised that they had reached the entrance to the sanctum. It was just like his vision. He looked at the expectant faces around him and realised that apart from the initial firing the moment they encountered the palace guard's, the aliens had not attacked again. Were the events from his vision being replayed? Had the alien's found an alternate route inside. "We need to move!" he shouted. "The invaders could already be inside!"

The Chaplain rushed over to the large double doors and pushed then open. He entered, trying not to look at the horrendous depictions of torture that were displayed on the walls. The Chaplain unholstered his weapon. He turned to face the wall. They hadn't come through yet, meaning they must still be in the tunnel.

Cladinus hurried up to him. He snatched the gun out of his hands then held onto his arm while all the others filed past them. "You have done well, Chaplain. Do not destroy the scheme by acting rash."

"What is going on here?" he cried.

The large alien pulled him out of the sanctum just as he heard the invaders breaking through that wall. "We have to stop them!"

Cladinus ignored his plea and just dragged the Chaplain through the hall. "Come, witness the dawn of a new age." The Gizanti dropped the man beside the sergeant at arms before taking up position a few metres behind Cole.

Apart from the ancient three sleep-pods in the middle of this magnificent room, everything else differed from the room he saw in his vision. The Chaplain could not understand the reason for the changes. Cole, Walish Din, and the girl looked to be in a trance as they walked over to the sleep-pods. They all gripped the sides and proceeded to climb inside.

This could not be right! Where was the God-Emperor? The central pillar then began to shimmer. Flecks of silver lifted from the surface and floated through the air. The silver continued to detach until all that was left was a clear cylinder full of a yellow fluid. A body moved within the fluid, but even the Chaplain could see that it was not the God-Emperor. The figure's eyes snapped open. They darted across each human and alien until they found the Chaplain. The figure's mouth opened impossibly wide before an ear-piercing scream filled the air.

The Chaplain dropped to the floor. "High Priestess. Please forgive me. I have sinned. Show mercy, show mercy."

He too shrieked when that central pillar exploded, covering the people in front of it with viscous liquid and thousands of crystal shards. The Chaplain slowly got to his feet, unable to take his eyes off the shivering, naked body lying at their feet.

The High Priestess managed to raise her head. She glared at the Gizanti warrior. "Foul alien filth," she hissed.

Cladinus simply looked over towards the main entrance. "Finish it," he commanded.

The Chaplain spun around. The three marines were framed in the doorway, all armed with the alien staff weapons.

Magnus took aim and fired. His blast turned the real ruler of the Terran Empire into crimson mush.

"What have I done?"

"You have helped to save your species from extinction," replied Cladinus. He then removed a cuboid object, walked up to the sleep-pods, and pushed it into the central base before turning back around. "Philip. I hope that one day you will forgive me and understand why this is necessary. Your species cannot be allowed to control so much power ever again."

Before any of them could react, the Gizanti grabbed the sides of the girl's head with his huge hands and savagely twisted. The alien then climbed into the waiting sleep-pod along with Cole and Walish Din.

The Chaplain managed to raise his gun, but before he could release a single blast, a yellow haze appeared around the three sleep-pods and enclosed the device and its occupants. The haze then solidified, creating an impenetrable shield.

# CHAPTER SIXTEEN

**Cole Aspect**

Once the connections were bonded and the three joined as one, he silently raged at the alien's duplicity, at diverting the true path to fit their design. Cole saw the Gizanti purposely using the girl to divert the drones so the Battle Sister could assess and duplicate her talent before inserting it into him. The alien would not have been able to enter the pod otherwise. He saw him give the three marines alternate commands as well as displacing the staff weapons to the surface. The Walish Din Aspect gave council and they both listened to the Cladinus Aspect explain his reasoning. His rage began displeasure until it settled down to grudging acceptance. What was done was done. The three had an eternity to further discuss the deception. Right now, the present needed rectifying.

Eight million pods had already left the incubators. The Cole Aspect nullified those before stopping any further displacement. He then returned the pods to their respective owners and began the reverse engineering process. It would take many weeks for the humans to be whole again. This pleased the Cole Aspect, for once they awoke, the many millions of humans upon those two planets would find themselves in paradise.

**Walish Din Aspect**

It took valuable time to find a compromise between the human and the Gizanti, in which many more of his people woke up on the plains of Gopin. He could not help those, but the Walish Din

Aspect would not allow any more to suffer. He dismantled the energy matrix around his planet and removed the one around the blue aliens' home at the same time. Every staff weapon in existence vanished. He also ensured every Terran hand weapon disappeared. From this moment on, every sentient species in the Galactic Expanse would not need to kill again.

## Cladinus Aspect

His species had suffered too much. With the help of the device he inserted into the base on this machine, he removed the shackles placed on his people and wiped their memories so none would carry the burden of the evil they administered whilst under the control of the invaders. He then turned his attention to the thousands of military Terran Mechs still heading towards the Imperial home planet. He could just as easily nullified every machine, but the Cladinus Aspect thought otherwise. Only half were changed back.

He chose a deserted planet and displaced every machine to the surface. The restored mechs immediately attacked the thousands of altered mechs.

The Cladinus Aspect then beamed the resulting carnage and mayhem to every display screen and monitor with the Galactic Expanse. This was how the Terran Empire would be remembered. Every sentient creature would understand that the new age, the one which was promised so long ago, was now here.

# THREE THOUSAND YEARS AGO

Until they arrived, almost everybody believed that the nightmare of nuclear war was just days away. The three superpowers had been at each other's throats for weeks. Mediation only exacerbated the conflict.

In the beginning, three massive starships entered Earth's orbit and took up position directly above the Whitehouse, the Kremlin, and Zhongnanhai.

Most of the planet breathed a sigh of relief, now believing that with the arrival of these beings from another planet, the superpowers would realise the error of their ways and halt the madness.

Many others secretly wondered if they had just swapped a very human war for alien invasion. Nobody knew what these alien monsters wanted from their planet, but they also questioned the timing of their arrival. It seemed a little too neat to be coincidental.

The superpowers did indeed reluctantly admit that perhaps their species had more pressing matters to attend before they annihilated their home.

For two weeks, the three ships hovered above their chosen locations. Every imaginable method of communication with the aliens proved ineffective. Some wondered if these vast ships were even inhabited.

The silence broke three days later when three solid black spheres, one from each vessel, floated down to the ground. They stayed there for a further three days, attracting crowds of millions. The black spheres became transparent, showing the whole world what lay inside. They looked in confusion at the sight of three ordinary-looking humans, one female and two male.

They said that the visitors had chosen them to lead the species into a new era of peace and prosperity. They possessed the knowledge to take them to the stars. They were no longer alone. The galaxy was alive, teeming with many wonderful sentient beings.

\*\*\*

Her own government had approached the chosen woman and made it clear that only they should possess the alien technology, that to allow the others access to such unimaginable power would cause another arms race, one which nobody could win.

She stood beside the machine built for them by the aliens which would give the three chosen God-like powers. The woman turned to her companions. She smiled at the pair of them before shooting the two men in the face.

# THE END

# CHECK OUT OTHER GREAT SCIENCE FICTION BOOKS

## SALVAGE MERC ONE
by Jake Bible

Joseph Laribeau was born to be a Marine in the Galactic Fleet. He was born to fight the alien enemies known as the Skrang Alliance and travel the galaxy doing his duty as a Marine Sergeant. But when the War ended and Joe found himself medically discharged, the best job ever was over and he never thought he'd find his way again.

Then a beautiful alien walked into his life and offered him a chance at something even greater than the Fleet, a chance to serve with the Salvage Merc Corp.

Now known as Salvage Merc One Eighty-Four, Joe Laribeau is given the ultimate assignment by the SMC bosses. To his surprise it is neither a military nor a corporate salvage. Rather, Joe has to risk his life for one of his own. He has to find and bring back the legend that started the Corp.

## SERENGETI
by J.B. Rockwell

It was supposed to be an easy job: find the Dark Star Revolution Starships, destroy them, and go home. But a booby-trapped vessel decimates the Meridian Alliance fleet, leaving Serengeti—a Valkyrie class warship with a sentient AI brain—on her own; wrecked and abandoned in an empty expanse of space. On the edge of total failure, Serengeti thinks only of her crew. She herds the survivors into a lifeboat, intending to sling them into space. But the escape pod sticks in her belly, locking the cryogenically frozen crew inside.

Then a scavenger ship arrives to pick Serengeti's bones clean. Her engines dead, her guns long silenced, Serengeti and her last two robots must find a way to fight the scavengers off and save the crew trapped inside her.

# CHECK OUT OTHER GREAT SCIENCE FICTION BOOKS

## MAUSOLEUM 2069
by **Rick Jones**

Political dignitaries including the President of the Federation gather for a ceremony onboard Mausoleum 2069. But when a cloud of interstellar dust passes through the galaxy and eclipses Earth, the tenants within the walls of Mausoleum 2069 are reborn and the undead begin to rise. As the struggle between life and death onboard the mausoleum develops, Eriq Wyman, a one-time member of a Special ops team called the Force Elite, is given the task to lead the President to the safety of Earth. But is Earth like Mausoleum 2069? A landscape of the living dead? Has the war of the Apocalypse finally begun? With so many questions there is only one certainty: in space there is nowhere to run and nowhere to hide.

## RED CARBON
by **D.J. Goodman**

Diamonds have been discovered on Mars.

After years of neglect to space programs around the world, a ruthless corporation has made it to the Red Planet first, establishing their own mining operation with its own rules and laws, its own class system, and little oversight from Earth. Conditions are harsh, but its people have learned how to make the Martian colony home.

But something has gone catastrophically wrong on Earth. As the colony leaders try to cover it up, hacker Leah Hartnup is getting suspicious. Her boundless curiosity will lead her to a horrifying truth: they are cut off, possibly forever. There are no more supplies coming. There will be no more support. There is no more mission to accomplish. All that's left is one goal: survival.

# CHECK OUT OTHER GREAT
# SCIENCE FICTION BOOKS

## IN PERPETUITY
by Jake Bible

For two thousand years, Earth and her many colonies across the galaxy have fought against the Estelian menace. Having faced overwhelming losses, the CSC has instituted the largest military draft ever, conscripting millions into the battle against the aliens. Major Bartram North has been tasked with the unenviable task of coordinating the military education of hundreds of thousands of recruits and turning them into troops ready to fight and die for the cause.

As Major North struggles to maintain a training pace that the CSC insists upon, he realizes something isn't right on the Perpetuity. But before he can investigate, the station dissolves into madness brought on by the physical booster known as pharma. Unfortunately for Major North, that is not the only nightmare he faces- an armada of Estelian warships is on the edge of the solar system and headed right for Earth!

## BATTLEFIELD MARS
by David Robbins

Several centuries into the future, Earth has established three colonies on Mars. No indigenous life has been discovered, and humankind looks forward to making the Red Planet their own.

Then 'something' emerges out of a long-extinct volcano and doesn't like what the humans are doing.

Captain Archard Rahn, United Nations Interplanetary Corps, tries to stem the rising tide of slaughter. But the Martians are more than they seem, and it isn't long before Mars erupts in all-out war.